A MAC McCLELLAN MYSTERY

DEADLY CATCH

E. MICHAEL
HELMS

SEVENTH STREET BOOKS™

AN IMPRINT OF PROMETHEUS BOOKS

59 JOHN GLENN DRIVE • AMHERST, NY 14228
www.seventhstreetbooks.com

Published 2013 by Seventh Street Books

Cover illustration © 2013 Media Bakery
Cover design by Grace Conti-Zilsberger

Inquiries should be addressed to
Seventh Street Books
59 John Glenn Drive
Amherst, New York 14228-2119
VOICE: 716-691-0133
FAX: 716-691-0137
WWW.PROMETHEUSBOOKS.COM

17 16 15 14 13   5 4 3 2 1

Library of Congress Cataloging-in-Publication Data

Helms, E. Michael.
    Deadly catch : a Mac McClellan mystery / E. Michael Helms.
        pages cm
    ISBN 978-1-61614-867-6 (pbk.)
    ISBN 978-1-61614-868-3 (ebook)
    1. Retired military personnel—Fiction. 2. Marines—Fiction. 3. Murder—
Investigation—Fiction. 4. Drug traffic—Fiction. 5. Florida Panhandle (Fla.)—
Fiction. I. Title. II. Title: Mac McClellan mystery.

PS3608.E4653D43 2013
813'.6—dc23

2013024952

Printed in the United States of America

For Karen

CHAPTER 1

The first cast of the day turned my dream vacation into a nightmare.

A quick flick of the wrist and the lure flashed in the rising sun, arched thirty or so yards alongside the grass flats and landed with a quiet splash barely a foot from the edge. Bull's-eye! During my week of fishing the waters of St. George Bay I'd developed a nice touch for casting, especially for someone who'd hardly wet a line the past twenty years. I closed the bail, gave the rod tip a couple of light twitches, and waited.

I'd hooked and landed some fine speckled trout the past few days, but I still hadn't nailed a bragging-size "gator" trout despite a crash course in speck fishing from Lamar Randall. Lamar is the mechanic and part-time fishing guide who keeps the rental boats at Gillman's Marina in tiptop condition. When I first met him he was wearing an eye patch, and with his goatee and longish hair he bore an uncanny resemblance to a classic Hollywood pirate. He'd recently suffered an injury while working on a boat he was building at home and would have to wear the protective patch for several more weeks.

Lamar is also known as one of the best trout and redfish anglers along the Florida Panhandle. When I'd asked why he was turning wrenches instead of guiding rich tourists full-time to his favorite honey-holes, he laughed.

"I got three kids and a wife to feed. Throw in bad weather, the slow winters, well, you get the picture. Now if I was still single . . ."

After a minute I gave the rod tip another twitch and began a slow retrieve. The lure wiggled and skirted the grassy edge for ten or fifteen feet when I felt resistance. My pulse raced as I yanked back on the rod to set the hook and started reeling. The rod bent against the heavy weight, and I got psyched for the fight of my angling life. Seconds later disappointment doused my adrenaline rush. Gator trout, my ass. I was hung up.

I lowered the rod, pointed the tip at whatever I'd snagged, and pulled, hoping to free the lure. No such luck. I tried again with the same results. Well, damned if I was going to give it up without a fight. I'd paid six ninety-five plus tax for that MirrOlure at the marina shop last evening. I lived just fine on my military retirement, but seven bucks was seven bucks. If it came down to it I'd swim for that lure.

After a few more tries I gave up trying to free the lure. It was stuck fast. The thought of getting wet this early in the morning didn't thrill me, but moving the boat closer to the grass flats would be more likely to spook whatever fish might be lurking around than my wading. Decision made, I released the bail to give the line some slack and leaned the spinning outfit against the gunnels. The clear water looked shallow enough, but just to be sure I grabbed the paddle from its rack. The handle slipped beneath the surface, and the water rose past my elbow before the blade struck bottom. With luck my head and neck would be above water.

I shed my shirt, kicked off my new leather deck shoes, emptied my pockets, and unclipped the cell phone from my belt. There wasn't much wind to speak of, but I knew that could change without warning. So, I crawled onto the bow, unfastened the anchor, slipped the rope through the bow guide and lowered it to the bottom. I gave the anchor line a few feet of slack and wrapped it fast to a cleat. I tugged on the 12-pound test monofilament again to relocate my target. Satisfied of my bearings, I braced my hands on the gunnels and hopped over the side.

The bay was chilly even though June was just a few days away. I stood there a minute getting used to the water, which topped out just below my shoulders. Then I headed for the grass flats using the "stingray shuffle" that Kate, the attractive saleslady at Gillman's, had demonstrated for me should I decide for whatever reason to go wading in these waters. A trip to the local emergency room to remove a stingray barb wasn't high on my vacation agenda.

I found the fishing line, held it loosely in my right hand, and eased along. I kept my eyes focused on where I thought the lure was, making as little motion as possible. About halfway to the target a light breeze rose and drifted my way. That's when the stench hit, almost gagging me. Iraq flashed through my mind, bodies rotting in the alleys and rubble of Fallujah. Whatever the hell I'd snagged had to be sizeable to raise that much stink. A dolphin or sea turtle, maybe a shark. Lamar had mentioned that this area of the bay was a prime breeding ground for certain species of sharks. Well, if this *was* a shark I smelled, it was in no condition to attack me.

I covered my mouth and nose with my free hand and kept going, breathing as little and shallow as possible. Just a few feet from my objective I lifted the line out of the water and gave it a light pull. Five feet away, the surface exploded. Hundreds of small fish and blue crabs darted and scurried in every direction. I tripped backward and nearly went under before I somehow regained my footing. My heart was racing, and despite the foul air I grabbed several deep breaths to calm myself. Then I saw it—my lure, embedded in the bleached-white underbelly of a large fish sticking halfway out of the grass.

"You chickenshit," I muttered, glad no fishing buddies were along to witness my brave reaction to a bunch of scavengers feasting on a dead fish. I turned my head and took another deep breath and covered the few remaining feet as fast as possible. Pulling the line tight, I reached for the lure. My hand froze in midair and I stumbled back again, heart pounding. Christ on a crutch, this was no dead fish! It was a leg—a human leg!

CHAPTER 2

I don't recall much about getting back to the boat, but you can bet your ass the stingray shuffle had no part in it. I grabbed the gunnels and heaved myself back aboard. I found a towel, dried my face, and ran it through my hair while I tried to calm down and think. Okay, I'd hooked a dead body. I needed to call . . . who? The sheriff's office, St. George police? I didn't have either number. 911? But this was no real emergency. Whatever—*whoever*—I'd snagged was way past needing medical attention.

Gillman's. I had the marina's number programmed in my phone in case I broke down or ran into some other kind of trouble. Well, this sure as hell qualified. I punched in the number and fished a beer from the ice chest.

"Gillman's Marina. How may I help you?"

I recognized the chatty voice. I swallowed a mouthful of beer and took a breath. "Kate, it's Mac McClellan."

"Morning, Mac. Having any luck?"

I took another swig. "Yeah, all bad. I—"

"Oh? Well, dang. Maybe we should've gone with the gold instead of—"

"No, it's not the lure."

"Motor trouble? Lamar just went through that motor a few weeks ago."

"No, listen. I was fishing the grass flats just off the island back of the Trade Winds Lodge a few minutes ago, and I . . . I hooked a body."

There was a pause. "A what?"

"A body. A dead human body."

"You sure?" Kate's voice had lost its chattiness. "I mean, you're sure it's not a dolphin or something?"

"It's a body."

There was another pause, longer this time. "Mac, I'm putting you on hold for a minute, okay? Don't hang up."

I'd finished my beer and was well into my second when Kate came back on the line. "Mac?"

"I'm here."

"I contacted Fish and Wildlife. They should have a boat there in a half hour or so. They said to stay put and don't touch anything."

I almost laughed out loud. "Tell 'em not to worry."

I switched on my portable radio and tried to pass the time watching a small flock of terns diving on a school of minnows while waiting for Fish and Wildlife to show up. But the music and bird watching weren't much help, and I'd damned near polished off a six-pack when I spotted a boat approaching from the mainland. This one was heading straight for me. Earlier, I'd seen a couple of others heading southwest, probably for fishing spots of their own. I'd been tempted to flag them down. I could've used the company but decided against it. Not much sense in screwing up their day with my troubles.

I took a quick glance over my shoulder again. The crabs had returned, and if I hadn't known what was out there, I wouldn't have a clue. I thought about the fried soft-shell crabs I'd had for dinner a few nights ago and felt my gut twist. Thank god for the wind change.

I turned my head and stared northeast at the approaching boat. I could barely make out the throaty hum of the outboard now. I finished my beer, crushed the can, and tossed it in the ice chest. I decided against popping another one. I didn't need a DUI or whatever the hell they call it for being inebriated on the water. But that was small potatoes compared to what was lying up in that grass.

I fished a roll of breath mints from my pocket and popped a couple in my mouth. It was warm now, and I'd dried out. Everything was back in place except for my shoes and sanity. How the hell could this be happening? I was on vacation, for christsake, a month out of the Marine Corps and looking forward to a long R&R before deciding what to do with the rest of my life. And now this. For the first time since my discharge I felt a twinge of regret that I hadn't re-upped for one more hitch with the Corps. Twenty-four years had been enough, I'd thought, but now I wasn't so sure.

When the boat was about fifty yards away I heard the motor throttle back. The bow dipped and swayed with the drop in power, then the boat straightened and approached at a no-wake speed. I recognized the Fish and Wildlife emblem on the hull. I returned the officer's wave and watched as he slid the gear handle into neutral. A second later he switched off the motor, his boat maybe ten yards astern and drifting closer.

"Morning," he called, leaving the steering station and stepping toward the bow. "Are you Mr. McClellan?"

"Yes, sir," I said to a trim, dark-haired officer I judged to be eight or ten years my junior—my formality a product of ingrained military habit I'd yet to shake. The gray and green uniform and nine-millimeter pistol strapped to his waist didn't help matters.

He stood just back of the bow, took off his cap, and wiped his forehead with the back of a hand. "Kate at Gillman's says we've got some trouble here."

"Yeah, I'd say so." I pointed behind me. "There's a body about thirty yards back there."

His boat drifted alongside mine. I grabbed hold of the bow and watched as he squinted in the general direction I'd pointed. "The crabs?"

"Yeah," I said, damned impressed with his eye for detail. I'd never noticed the crabs before they'd bolted, nearly scaring the life out of me.

"Okay then," he said, still staring ahead, "climb aboard. "Let's go take a look."

"Call me Mac," I said, after he'd identified himself as Officer Dave Reilly, Florida Fish and Wildlife. I sat on the starboard bow of the twenty-foot Mako while Dave stood portside and used a long pole he'd grabbed from a rack to push us toward the target. Damned if I wanted any part of messing with that body. I'd seen more than enough already. As a First Sergeant in the Marines with a sleeve full of lifer stripes, I'd been used to ordering shave-tail lieutenants around. But I was a civilian now and more than happy to let Officer Reilly handle things from here on out.

"Tell me again exactly what you saw," Dave said, when we were about halfway to the corpse.

I repeated how I'd made my cast, how I thought I'd hooked a big speck, realized I was hung up, and then what I'd found when I tried to retrieve my lure.

"And you're positive it's a body, not some fish or animal."

I exhaled sharply. First Kate, now this guy. "Look, I fought in Desert Storm and did two combat tours during Iraqi Freedom. I've seen more dead than I care to remember. I'm positive."

Dave nodded, kept his eyes focused ahead and pushed on. "Sorry, Mac. It's just that I've been in on a few too many drowning recoveries and I'm not looking forward to this."

"Join the crowd," I said, as the wind shifted and the stench hit us full in the face.

Dave coughed, almost gagged. "God."

My gut flipped in agreement. "Yeah, it's a ripe one."

He stopped the boat, then eased the pole toward the body until the scavengers scattered. From my perch on the bow I could make out both legs and the buttocks of a body, badly swollen and partially eaten. The upper half was entangled and covered by the grass, though patches of bleached-white flesh showed through here and there.

Dave coughed and spit, then started poling fast toward the beach. Only when we were well past and upwind of the body did he slow down. "I'll call this in when we get ashore. There's nothing we can do back there. Headquarters will send out a team and the medical examiner if he's available. This is outside St. George's jurisdiction, so the county's got to be called in on this, too."

I assumed he meant the Palmetto County Sheriff's Department whose headquarters was in Parkersville, the county seat, about six miles by land west of St. George. "What about my boat?"

Dave glanced my way. "I'll get you back to your boat, but they'll have to search the area and recover the body first," he said, poling through a channel that cut through the grass flats twenty yards from shore. "And they're going to want to question you, of course. That body was naked. I doubt it's a routine drowning."

"Yeah, so I noticed," I said, wondering if Officer Reilly had ever heard of skinny dipping. I'd sobered up quickly, but right then I could've used another beer or two. "What'll they want with me? I've already told you everything I know."

I lurched forward as the boat scraped bottom. Dave dropped the pole, grabbed a coiled anchor line, swung it like a grappling hook, and tossed it onto the beach. He turned to me, hands resting on hips.

"As far as I know, there haven't been any reports of missing persons around here for a while." He pointed toward the body. "An unclothed floater that's been in the water for several days, I'd estimate, and you found the body, Mac. Until we know better, my guess is the sheriff will treat this as a crime scene."

"So, what's that got to do with me?"

"Kate said you've been in the area for the past week. Knowing Sheriff Pickron, I'd say there's a good chance he'll find that an interesting coincidence."

CHAPTER 3

The natives of Palmetto County differ as to how Five-Mile Island got its name. It lies roughly five miles off the coast of the Florida Panhandle. It also happens to be approximately five miles long. Take your pick. Running east to west, it forms a natural barrier that protects the fishing-turned-artsy-village of St. George, and the bay's rich oyster and scallop beds many of the locals still depend upon for their livelihood. The pork chop–shaped island is about a hundred yards wide at its eastern juncture where it joins a bridge and causeway leading to the mainland. It widens gradually as you travel west, the last two-mile stretch being Five-Mile Island State Park, a beautiful area of wide sugar-white beaches and towering dunes on the Gulf of Mexico. Inland, bent, and weathered stands of scrub oak give way to native longleaf pines that, a mile later, surrender to small dunes and a narrow beach that skirts the fertile waters of St. George Bay.

There are a hundred or so seasonal or full-time residences strung out from the causeway to the park entrance, a convenience store/gas station, a couple of mom-and-pop motels, and the Trade Winds Lodge. The Trade Winds is the gem of the island, consisting of a turn-of-the-twentieth-century two-story wooden hotel overlooking the gulf, a dozen rental cabins along the bay, a gift shop, and a decent restaurant. I'd stayed at the lodge a couple of nights when I first arrived in the area, but when I decided to hang around a while and try my luck fishing, I'd rented a camping space at Gulf Pines Campground in St. George. Twenty-five bucks a night beat a hundred-fifty all day long, despite the sacrifice in comfort. Besides, my twenty-two-foot Grey Wolf camping trailer was plenty swanky for me. I'd spent too many nights in foxholes to complain about any lack of luxury.

After the Fish and Wildlife team showed up to secure the scene, Dave and I waited inside the restaurant with a couple of Cokes escaping the noon heat. Twenty minutes later Sheriff Pickron pulled into the parking lot in a white, unmarked Jeep SUV. Two green-and-white county squad cars quickly followed, along with a utility van marked Palmetto County Dive & Rescue. Through the window I saw the sheriff climb out of the SUV, point to the bay, and mouth orders to several deputies. They scrambled to gather dive gear and other equipment from the van, and then disappeared down the path leading to the cabins.

Pickron was all brawn, built like an NFL linebacker. He nearly filled the doorway when he stepped inside the restaurant. He took off his sunglasses and glanced around, then headed for our table. On his way over I heard a couple of patrons greet him as "Bo," or the more formal "Sheriff Bo." Our waitress, a thirty-something, bottled-blonde looker, was all smiles as she intercepted him with a friendly pat on the shoulder, and then hurried away with his order.

"Reilly," Pickron said, nodding as he pulled out the chair next to Dave.

"Sheriff," Dave said, "this is Mac McClellan. He found the body."

I reached across the table and we shook hands as the waitress brought a sweating glass of iced tea and set it down with a couple of napkins.

"Y'all need anything else, just holler," she said and sashayed off to another table.

The sheriff took the slice of lemon from the rim of his glass and squeezed it into the tea, then stirred it with a meaty finger, ignoring the teaspoon inside the glass. "So McClellan, what brings you to our little piece of paradise?" His deep voice struck me as hovering somewhere between unfriendly and bullying.

"A buddy I served with in the Marines used to brag about the fishing here," I said, a little irked by his brusqueness. "I retired a few weeks back. I've got some time on my hands, so I decided to come down and check it out."

What might pass for a grin crept across the sheriff's bulldoggish face. He swiped a hand across his buzz-cut hair. "Gyrene, huh? I was Army, myself. Chopper pilot. Ever hear of Somalia?" From his tone I was leaning toward bullying.

"Yeah. *Black Hawk Down* and all that. Not one of our finest hours," I said, now a little beyond irked.

His grin faded into a frown. He reached in his shirt pocket and pulled out a small notebook and pen. "That friend of yours, I'd like his name and current residence in case I need to check out your story."

"Staff Sergeant Jeffrey Sanderson, Arlington National Cemetery," I said, looking the sheriff square in the eye. "But I doubt you'll get much out of him."

Sheriff Pickron flushed and his jaw tightened. He grabbed his glass of tea and downed it in a few gulps. "I got an investigation to oversee," he said, sliding his chair back and standing. He turned and eyeballed me. "You mind if we take a look at your boat?"

I hesitated, rolling the cool glass between my palms.

"I can get a warrant," Pickron said, almost a snarl.

"Go ahead; I've got nothing to hide."

"You stay put until I say otherwise," he said, meaning me, then turned and strode out the door.

"That wasn't very wise," Dave said after the sheriff stormed out of the restaurant. "Bo Pickron's considered a hero around these parts. He won the Distinguished Flying Cross in Somalia. Getting on his bad side won't sit well with folks in this county."

"Yeah, well, I don't like getting pushed around, even with words." I waved the waitress over and ordered a draft Bud for me and another Coke for Dave. "How long has he been sheriff?"

Dave shrugged and stared at the melting ice in the bottom of his glass. "I'd say about a year or two after he got out of the Army. 'Ninety-five, 'ninety-six, I'd guess. His daddy was sheriff before him."

"Yeah? A regular dynasty."

"I guess you could call it that. His brother-in-law has been mayor of St. George for the last ten years or so."

A familiar image flashed through my mind. "George Harper, the real estate tycoon?" I'd seen "Friendly George's" grinning mug plastered on billboards all over Palmetto County.

"That's him."

The waitress brought our drinks, set mine on the table with a less-than-delicate thud, and left without offering so much as a smile.

"Looks like word's getting around already," I said. I held up and eyeballed the frosted mug of beer. "You think it's safe to drink this?"

Dave chuckled. "Loretta's got a thing for Bo, but I doubt she'd resort to poisoning for him. She's got way too much competition to be that drastic."

Twenty minutes later an ambulance pulled up, no lights or siren to signal its arrival. A couple of EMTs got out, walked around back, and opened the doors. They pulled out a gurney and rolled it down the path toward the bay. Dave and I finished our drinks and walked outside for a better look.

Down by the bay, four F and W officers wearing rubber gloves and breathing masks lugged a white body bag up the hill. Sheriff Pickron and two men in wetsuits followed close behind. When they met up with the EMTs they placed the body onto the gurney. The EMTs strapped it down, then a couple of officers pushed while the EMTs pulled the load up the path. Reaching the parking lot, they rolled the gurney to the ambulance and loaded it. After a few words with the sheriff, the EMTs climbed into the ambulance and drove off toward the causeway.

The men in wetsuits headed back downhill toward the bay as Bo Pickron walked up to Dave and me, his face a bit pale and looking none too happy. He scowled at me and held up a clear plastic bag containing what looked to be a folded, black-handled pocketknife.

"Ever see this before, McClellan?"

I took the bag from his hand and looked closely. It was a Buck, and I had indeed seen it before. *Mac* was inscribed on the stainless steel butt, a gift from my ex-wife a few years back, before she ditched me to "find herself."

I felt the right cargo pocket of my shorts. It was empty. I'd forgotten all about the knife when I'd emptied my shorts to go wading. "Yeah, it's mine," I said, slipping my hand into the pocket to find a small hole in the corner of the net material.

"You mind telling me how it wound up under the body?"

I glanced at Dave and handed the bag back to the sheriff. "It's like I told Officer Reilly. I snagged something with my lure and went wading to retrieve it. When the crabs scattered and I saw it was a body, I stumbled backward. The knife must've slipped through this hole in my pocket." I turned the net pocket inside out and pushed my finger through the hole. "I don't know, maybe I kicked it when it fell out."

Pickron snorted. He seemed unconvinced by my story. "And you say you've got no idea how the body got there?"

"That's what I'm saying."

The sheriff tossed the bag to a deputy standing nearby. He crossed his arms across his chest, trying to look more intimidating, I guessed. "You realize what the odds are that you'd motor across the bay to this particular spot, make your first cast of the day, and just happen to snag a body? A million to one, maybe?"

I'd just about had enough of this bull crap for one day. "Look, Sheriff, I'm no statistician, but if I had anything to do with this, then why the hell would I sink my lure in the body, plant my pocketknife under it, and call the law? I can think up a couple of dozen better alibis than that."

We sparred back and forth the next few minutes. Finally I asked him if I was under arrest.

"No, but this isn't over yet, not by a long shot. We got an autopsy coming up. You better not even think about leaving the county."

"Gulf Pines Campground, Sheriff, site 44. I'll be around."

~

It was after four before Sheriff Pickron gave the okay for Dave Reilly to ferry me out to my boat. Even then, we had to detour around a wide area marked by yellow crime-scene tape attached to small buoys

F and W had staked out to search for evidence. A larger orange buoy indicated the body's former location. Divers were still snorkeling in and around the grass flats.

I stepped off his boat and onto mine and gave my boat a quick survey. The spinning combo I'd used when I hooked the body was missing. Good thing I had backups. My tackle box was open and a jumbled mess. It would take a couple of hours to straighten things out after their thorough search. The batteries were removed from my radio and lay scattered across the deck, but everything else aboard seemed to be in place. I hoisted and secured the anchor, then fired up the motor and slowly pulled away toward the mainland. Dave followed alongside for a short distance, then waved and gunned his Mako toward Parkersville where the Fish and Wildlife headquarters was located.

Dark clouds were building in the northwest, and distant jags of lightning cut the sky. I opened up the throttle and made good time for about a mile until the wind shifted and the boat began bucking waves. I throttled back a bit and changed course so that I was heading a little west of the marina. That made for a smoother ride, though it would likely add several minutes to my return trip.

I made decent time for another mile or so until the wind increased and it began to rain. I had to cut back on the throttle even more to compensate for the rougher, blue-black seas. The wind seemed to be arguing with itself over which way to blow, and I found myself playing the wheel like I was driving on a winding mountain road. The rain was pelting now. I grabbed my phone, shielding it from the downpour the best I could. Gripping the wheel with one hand, I punched in Gillman's number.

"Gillman's, this is Kate, how may I help you?"

Being tossed about on an angry sea reminded me of why I'd joined the Marines and not the Navy or Air Force. I'd always felt more comfortable with my feet planted on solid ground, even when people were shooting at me. I figured when the shit hit the fan my chances of survival were better on terra firma than sinking to Davy Jones's locker or falling out of the sky like a rock. Kate's calm greeting relieved some of the tension this greenhorn mariner was feeling.

"Kate, it's Mac. It's getting rough out here. Any idea what's up with this weather?" There had been no indication of bad weather in the report I'd gotten before I'd left the marina that morning.

"Hold on a minute, Mac, I've got another call."

Kate wasn't the only one busy. I pressed the heel of my phone hand onto the wheel to help turn hard left, keeping the bow pointed toward a three- to four-foot oncoming swell. The boat lifted over the wave and steadied. I put the phone back to my ear.

"Mac . . . Mac, you there?"

"Yeah."

"Where are you?"

"I'm about halfway between the island and you, heading a little west to keep into the sea."

"That's good. I just checked NOAA radar. The squall's not too bad. It should blow by in another fifteen or twenty minutes. Try to keep your bow facing the waves and keep your throttle up as much as you can without taking on water. You don't want to get turned sideways in the trough."

"Roger that," I said, resisting the urge to preface it with *No shit!* "Thanks, Kate. See you when I get in, if I'm not too late."

"We'll be open till all the boats are in. Hey, how did things go with the . . . you know."

Another big swell was approaching. "Let's talk later. I'm a little busy right now."

⟞⟝

Kate proved to be a good prognosticator. If she ever wanted a job at The Weather Channel she could count on me for a recommendation. Twenty minutes later the storm blew by and I was under patchy blue skies with calming seas. To the east and south the squall was still raising hell.

Two or three hundred yards from shore the waves had died down enough that I was able to turn east and head parallel along the beach for the marina. A flight of brown pelicans passed low overhead, returning from whatever refuge they'd sought from the storm. They dipped and glided just above the wave tops, their wingtips acting like a blind man's cane. A small school of bottlenose dolphin appeared off my starboard and rode shotgun with me for a while, until they tired of the game and disappeared.

The storm had forced my boat farther west than I'd thought, and it was a good thirty minutes before I sighted the seawall that protected the mouth of the canal. A line from Robert Louis Stevenson's "Requiem" ran through my mind as I turned past the seawall into the slick calm waters of the canal. "*Home is the sailor, home from the sea . . .*" It was good to be back.

I cut the throttle to just above idle and relaxed, more than happy to obey the many *No Wake* signs nailed to the wooden walkways skirting both sides of Canal Park. The canal was lined with sheltered picnic tables. I waved at a resilient older couple sitting in lawn chairs, fishing rods at the ready. Gulls and pelicans stood atop pilings, preening and drying their feathers from the recent downpour. My stomach growled as the scent of barbeque drifted from a couple of the ritzy houses built near the canal. After what I'd seen earlier, I was surprised to find I still had an appetite. I grabbed a beer from the cooler and popped the top.

I steered the boat between the support pilings of the Highway 98 bridge and made the sharp right turn where the canal ran behind the marina. I motored past several occupied docking spaces until I came to number 14, then cut the motor and eased the boat into the slip. After securing the bow and stern lines, I stowed my gear, gathered up the day's trash, and stepped onto the dock, surprised to find my legs a little wobbly. I checked my watch. Six-thirty. Considering the storm, I'd made decent time. I finished my beer, tossed the can and handful of trash into a nearby container, and headed up the wooden stairway toward the marina store.

Wisps of steam rose from the asphalt parking lot. Glancing across the bay, I could barely make out the island. The sky there was dark and angry, and heavy rain clouds hung low over the horizon. A pickup truck drove by the front of the store. I waited for it to pass, sidestepped a puddle, pulled open the heavy glass door, and stepped inside.

Bells jingled and the wooden floor creaked under my deck shoes. Kate glanced up from behind the counter where she was waiting on a customer. She flashed a quick smile, her shoulder-length auburn hair shining under the fluorescent lighting. It was past normal closing time for a weekday, but a few customers still wandered about the store looking at tackle or souvenirs or clothing. I cut through the aisles to the back of the store, grabbed a Budweiser longneck from the cooler, and sat on a swivel deck chair in the boating accessories department. It had been a long, grueling day, and I was whipped mentally and physically. One thing months of combat had taught me was to grab shuteye when and where you could. Before I knew it, I'd dozed off.

I jolted awake, striking out with both hands and sloshing beer across the floor.

"Sorry, Mac! I didn't mean to scare you." Kate stared wide-eyed at me, keeping a safe distance away. "I was about to close up and saw you sitting here."

"Jesus, I'm sorry." My hands were shaking. I'd come close to punching her lights out, and it scared the hell out of me. These damn startle responses had ridden my ass like a monkey ever since Iraq. "You got a towel or something I can use to mop up this beer?"

"You sit tight," she said. "I'll take care of it."

I watched as Kate walked back into the main room and grabbed a roll of paper towels from behind the counter. I tried not to dwell on the way her jeans fit like a second skin, or how the Irish-green *Gillman's Marina* polo did little to hide her topside assets. The store appeared to be empty except for the two of us. In a minute she was back, kneeling a few feet away, swabbing the deck with a handful of towels.

"Sorry about all the mess," I said. "Be glad to help."

Kate looked up and smiled. It was the first time I'd noticed the tiny gap separating her front teeth. And for someone who'd lived her entire thirty-something years on the Gulf Coast, there was hardly a wrinkle to show for it. "Just about finished," she said. "Besides, you've had a dang rough day of it, I'd guess."

I swigged down what was left of the foamy beer. "I've had better."

Kate stood and tossed the wad of damp towels into a trash can. "You made the five-thirty news, Mac."

"Christ, that's all I need. What did they say?"

She dried her hands on a clean towel and tossed it into the trash. "Not much; just a quick report that an unidentified tourist discovered a body while fishing somewhere on the bay side of the island."

I took a deep breath and let it out slowly. "Any word on the body?"

Kate walked over and sat in a deck chair near me. The fluorescent lights made a few freckles stand out across her nose and cheeks. She shook her head. "No, nothing, not even if it was male or female."

I could sense the question in her eyes. "Then you know as much as me. All I saw was the legs and butt. It was in pretty bad shape."

"Was Bo Pickron there?"

Kate's question caught me a little off guard. "Oh, yeah, he was there all right. We didn't exactly hit it off like bosom buddies."

She gave a little laugh. "Now why on earth doesn't that surprise me?"

I recognized sarcasm when I heard it. I locked eyes with hers, noting they were nearly the same shade as her shirt. "You know the sheriff?"

"In this town, everybody knows everybody."

I couldn't help thinking she was being evasive, but I didn't want to push I held up the Bud bottle. "I could use another beer. Can I buy you one?"

Her eyebrows arched a little, and she nodded. "Sure, thanks. But let's take it outside. I need to lock up."

I got up and grabbed two Buds from the cooler. I handed one to Kate, then pulled six bucks out of my wallet and laid it next to the cash register as we walked by.

"You want a word of advice, Mac?" Kate said as she locked the double doors behind us.

"Shoot."

"Steer clear of Bo Pickron. He can be trouble."

CHAPTER 4

I decided to take a day off from fishing, so the next morning I slept in, if six a.m. qualifies for sleeping in. Thanks to the military, I'm an early riser. I got up, put on a pot of coffee, then walked to the campground store and bought a copy of the *Parkersville Independent* from the rack out front.

Back at the camper I poured myself a mug of strong black coffee, took a seat at the table, and opened the paper. There was nothing on the front page about the incident, so I flipped to the local/state section.

There it was: *Body discovered near Five-Mile Island*. It was barely a half-column long and provided little more dope than Kate's rundown of last evening's newscast. One bit of new information the article mentioned was that the unidentified victim was a female of undetermined age due to the body's deteriorated condition. The county medical examiner had been called in, and an autopsy was scheduled for some time today. Pending further investigation, the sheriff's office refused to comment on whether the apparent drowning was accidental or the result of foul play.

My name wasn't mentioned. I wasn't sure if that was a good thing or not. I wouldn't have to dodge questions from everybody and their cousin for a while until word got around, which I knew it soon would, but at the same time I wondered why Bo Pickron hadn't let the media know who discovered the body. After all, I had nothing to hide. Did the sheriff think that if my name went public I'd haul ass before the autopsy results were in? That didn't make much sense to me, but then again, neither did his theory that I might've dumped the body in the grass flats and then called the law to report I'd found it, conveniently leaving my inscribed pocketknife near the corpse as incriminating evidence. Pickron's attitude toward me didn't add up. Maybe he was just a natural prick.

I set the paper aside and fixed myself some scrambled eggs and toast. Later, I planned to drive to Gillman's and see if Kate might be able to wrangle any information from Fish and Wildlife or the sheriff's office. I'd only known her a little more than a week, but in that brief time I could tell she was one sharp lady and a real go-getter. If anyone could find out what was going on behind the scenes, it was Kate Bell.

Our talk over the beers last evening was the first time we'd exchanged more than just a few casual words, other than yesterday's phone conversations after I'd made my grisly discovery. Kate let me know that she appreciated the way I respected her opinion. When I first rented the boat and was looking at tackle to gear up for speckled trout fishing, Kate had waited on me. I'd accepted her recommendations with few questions, and that pleased her. She'd been around the fishing and tackle business most of her life. Her father had owned a tackle shop in Destin, some seventy-five miles west of St. George. Kate had worked in the family business since she was a kid, until one night a hurricane came calling and destroyed Bell's Tackle. Nearing retirement age at the time, her dad had chosen not to rebuild. A few years later Kate moved to St. George, answered a help-wanted ad and was hired on the spot by Gary and Linda Gillman.

Kate's biggest pet peeve was that when it came to fishing, most males—young, old, and in-between—refused to take her at her word. She'd lost track of the times she offered a customer sound advice, only to watch the guy seek out one of the male employees once her back was turned. Nine times out of ten the customer would receive the same suggestions Kate had offered. She was no closet feminist, but that sort of chauvinist behavior really goaded her. If I had an "in" with Kate, I figured it was because I'd recognized she knew her way around the fishing business.

Kate also let me know that she'd dated Bo Pickron not long after moving to St. George three years ago. Bo pulled her over one night in Parkersville, supposedly because of a burned-out tag light. Kate agreed to meet for a drink the next evening after work, and things had pro-gressed from there. After a few months she'd broken it off, though she didn't offer any explanation and I didn't press the matter. I had no idea why she even volunteered that information. Maybe it had something to do with her advice to steer clear of Pickron, or maybe, for whatever reason, she'd taken a liking to me. I'd never given Kate any indication that I was trying to hit on her, at least not consciously.

The truth is, I'd been burned out on women since I returned from my last overseas deployment and my loving wife greeted me with the happy news that she wanted a divorce. Sucker-punched, and just like that, twenty years shot to shit. At least Jill had had the decency to wait until the twins were ready to leave the nest. Mike was on a base-ball scholarship at UNC Wilmington, where he was the Seahawks' starting catcher. Megan was attending NC State with plans to enter their College of Veterinary Medicine once she acquired the necessary credits.

The kids had handled our split as well as could be expected and seemed to have adjusted to the situation. Jill and I pledged to remain on good terms for their sake, though deep down I sometimes felt like wringing her pretty little neck. *Semper Fidelis* is a trait that rates near the top in my book of mores.

As for my part, Kate got the abbreviated version: divorced, recently retired from the Marines, a couple of kids in college, and taking a few weeks of vacation while I figure out what to do with the rest of my life. Short, if not so sweet.

I pulled into the marina lot and parked in a spot well away from the palm tree a pair of maniacal mockingbirds had chosen to build their nest in and raise their young. On my first visit to Gillman's, the feathered dive bombers had nearly knocked the cap off my head. Respect earned, lesson learned.

I stepped into the store to the sound of tinkling bells. A couple of women were browsing the clothing racks, the only customers I noticed. Sara, the Gillmans' pretty teenage daughter, was manning the front counter. She'd been working the day I rented the boat and had handled the transaction like a pro. I returned her smile and wave, and walked over.

"Skipping school, huh?" I said, trying to sound intimidating.

"Noooo, Mr. Mac," she said in a cute Southern drawl devoid of any trace of her parents' Minnesotan lineage. "School's out already. Wednesday was our last day. Can I help you?"

I reached for my wallet, pleased Sara remembered me; a good sign for the upcoming generation that too often takes a bad rap. "I'd like to rent the boat for another week."

"Yes, sir." She disappeared a moment as she ducked behind the counter, then popped up like a blonde jack-in-the-box. She flipped through some pages of a ledger, then traced down with an index finger. "Slip 14, right?"

"Yes, ma'am," I said, happy to return the courtesy. Outside the Corps, I'd found it an all too rare commodity these days.

Her cheeks flushed a bit. "Cash or credit?"

I signed the rental extension Sara handed me, then the receipt after she'd run the card. "Is Kate around?"

"No, sir, she's off today." She brushed a strand of hair from her pale-blue eyes. "I could take a message if it's important."

"No, that's okay."

As I climbed back in my Chevy Silverado and started the engine, I wondered if Sara knew about yesterday's incident. If she did, she hadn't let it slip, but she might've just been being polite. Word always spreads fast in a small town.

I didn't have Kate's personal phone number, nor did I know where she lived. She hadn't offered, I hadn't asked, and I didn't want to put Sara in an uncomfortable position by asking her. I slipped the truck into drive and turned onto the highway, deciding it was time to pay a visit to the St. George Police Department.

Police headquarters was located three blocks off the highway in a small brick extension built onto the back of City Hall. A guy could pay his water bill or turn himself in to the law by walking just a few steps in one direction or the other. I stepped through the doorway into a small room painted drab beige. A few empty chairs lined one wall, several "wanted" or "missing persons" posters were tacked to a corkboard mounted on the opposite wall. The floor was covered in worn linoleum tile.

Behind the low counter sat a young lady who couldn't be a day older than my Megan, if that. She was busy typing into a computer, gum popping as her fingers worked over the keyboard. A radio, scanner, and mike sat near the computer, the radio hissing an occasional word or bit of chatter too indistinct for me to make out. She glanced up as I approached. *Beth* was monogrammed in cursive above the left-breast pocket of her white blouse.

"Can I help you?" Beth was all business, not offering even a hint of a smile. At first glance she'd seemed a bit on the plain side, but up close I saw potential.

"I'd like to see Chief Merritt, if he's in." I'd noticed the chief's name mentioned several times during my morning coffee/newspaper ritual.

For a few seconds Beth stared as though she hadn't heard me. "Name?"

"McClellan. Mac McClellan."

Her eyes lit up, the first show of expression since I'd walked through the door. She picked up the phone and punched a button. "Yes, sir, there's a Mr. McClellan here to see you."

Beth placed the phone back in its cradle. "The chief'll see you now. Through that door yonder," she said, pointing to the right of the counter.

I thanked her and walked to the door. *Chief Benjamin Merritt* was spelled out in gold lettering on a black plaque. I grabbed the handle and gave the door a couple of light raps.

"Come on in," came the gruff reply.

I stepped into his carpeted office and closed the door. A window air conditioner hummed from a side wall where concrete blocks had been cut out to accommodate the unit. The chief stood up behind a stout metal desk and greeted me with a handshake and friendly smile that belied his voice.

"Mr. McClellan. I expected we'd be meeting soon. Heard you had quite a catch yesterday."

"Yeah, you could say that, but nothing I'd want to keep." My gaze drifted to the wall behind. Several framed certificates were arranged in neat order, along with photos of the chief hobnobbing with what I supposed were local dignitaries. A certificate of commendation from the United States Air Force stood out from the rest.

"Have a seat," he said, motioning to a chair in front of the desk as he settled his husky frame back onto a padded swivel chair. There was a hint of gray streaking his short brown hair, and from the lines creasing his face I guessed he was on the back side of fifty.

"Call me Mac," I said, hoping to break the ice. "I was wondering if you have any information about what happened yesterday."

"Okay, Mac it is." A hint of a grin turned up the corners of his mouth. "My friends call me Ben, but you can call me Chief Merritt for now."

I wasn't sure if he thought I was patronizing him, or if he was testing me or what. Was this guy feeding from Bo Pickron's trough? One prick in a town this size was plenty to contend with.

"Do you have any information or leads on the victim, Chief Merritt?" I said, emphasizing his title and name. "Like how she might've ended up behind the Trade Winds Lodge?"

Merritt didn't answer; he just sat there staring at me, like he was trying to size me up.

I'd run up against this same pecking order bull while dealing with desk jockey officers more times than I cared to remember, and it never failed to rankle me. "Have there been any missing person reports lately, or boating accidents?"

The chief leaned forward and rested both arms on the desk. His eyes burned into mine for a moment, than he burst out laughing. "Twenty years in the Marines, right, Mac? Retired as a First Sergeant."

"Twenty-four." I knew now he'd done his homework checking up on me, probably at Sheriff Pickron's request.

"I pulled thirty in the Air Force myself. Chief Master Sergeant. Welcome back to civilian life."

"Thanks," I said, wondering where this conversation was heading. "What about the case?"

He leaned back, the chair creaking under the load. "Why all the interest? You found the body and reported it. I'd say you performed your civic duty."

"I wish you'd tell that to the sheriff. He practically accused me of dumping the body there."

"I heard they found your pocketknife near the body, but come on."

"Yeah. He bagged it for evidence. Acted like he thinks it might be the murder weapon."

Merritt snickered and shook his head. "Bocephus Pickron is a pompous ass."

It was my turn to laugh. "Bocephus? Are you serious?"

Merritt nodded. "Serious as I'm sitting here. His daddy was a big Hank Williams fan. If Bocephus was good enough for old Hank's boy, it was certainly good enough for his own."

"What about his war record? I heard he was some kind of hero chopper pilot in Somalia."

"Well, don't go believing everything you hear, especially when it comes to Bo Pickron. Look, this is off the record, okay? It's just my opinion, but that man would be lucky to be reading meters for the city if it wasn't for his family connections."

The laughs and banter had been a nice diversion, but it was time to get back to business. "What *do* you know about the case, Chief?"

"Not much, since it's county jurisdiction. They're performing the autopsy today. It'll be a while before we know the results. From what I hear, the victim was crab bait; no fingerprints or other identifiable body marks left. They're sending the dental records over the wire to see if they get lucky and come up with a match. The sheriff might have more, being it's in his ball park, but that's all I got. If I hear anything new, I'll let you know."

I stood up to leave and we shook hands again. "I appreciate it. Thanks for the info."

"Say Mac, we got a fine VFW post in town. Let's grab a beer sometime, vet to vet."

"Sounds good," I said, wondering if he was patronizing *me*.

"And call me Ben."

Later that afternoon I stopped back by Gillman's to get the boat prepped for a weekend of fishing. I'd thought over my talk with Ben Merritt and still wasn't sure how to read him. Which man was the real St. George Chief of Police—the stern, all-business "you can call me Chief Merritt," or the buddy-buddy "let's have a beer and call me Ben?"

I decided what he'd said made sense. I *had* done my civic duty by reporting the body. Beyond that, what business was it of mine? I'd been unlucky enough to stumble across the victim, but other than that the matter was over as far as I was concerned. The autopsy would surely clear up matters and remove any wild hair Bo Pickron had up his ass that I was involved in any way. I had a vacation to enjoy.

Lamar topped off the fuel tanks while I policed up the boat and made sure my tackle was in order. I was restocking my cooler with beer and ice when Lamar walked over with his chart of St. George Bay.

"Where you thinking about fishing tomorrow?" he said, squatting on the dock and looking over the chart with his good eye.

"Anywhere, as long as it's nowhere near the Trade Winds."

By now the word was out about my discovery. I'd fielded at least a dozen questions from the staff and customers since arriving at the marina a half hour earlier. I was sick of the whole business.

"Why don't you try The Stumps? It's about three miles west of the Lodge, near the park boundary. Usually holds some fine trout and redfish."

"Yeah? Any dead bodies lurking around?"

Lamar laughed. "Man, I'm sorry about that. That's the first time I ever put anybody on one of those."

I agreed to give The Stumps a try in the morning. Lamar marked it on my chart and gave me instructions about where to cast and what lures to try. "If you don't get any specks to take your topwaters, try a stingray grub. There's some honker reds that hang around them stumps. Flounder, too."

I gave Lamar a hard look. "No bodies, though. Your tip's riding on it."

I set out the next morning just after daybreak. I cleared the canal, eased over the shallow sandbar, and gunned the motor. It promised to be a beautiful day: few clouds, mild temps, and calm seas. Gulls wheeled high overhead on the rising currents, their raucous laughter welcoming the new day. To the east I saw a pod of dolphin swimming in a hunting circle, rustling up their morning meal.

I made good time, and before long the tall pines of Five-Mile Island State Park came into view. I checked my chart and steered a little to the east, keeping my eyes peeled for the dead tree trunks sticking out of the water that marked The Stumps. Decades ago a violent storm had cut a small spit of land off from the rest of the island. Over time the isolated mini-island had gradually eroded, until a once-vibrant stand of pines was inundated by salt water and died. Voilà, The Stumps.

Another twenty minutes, and I had The Stumps in sight. Slowing to a crawl, I maneuvered the boat to the east side of the dead forest and cut the motor. I dropped anchor, playing out about fifteen feet of line before it hit bottom, then wrapped the line around a bow cleat and got ready for some fishing.

The angling gods were smiling. Using a Rapala broken-back floating minnow, I soon had my limit of five speckled trout in the live well, all within the legal fifteen- to twenty-inch size. I'd also released another five or six that didn't measure up. I glanced at my watch and saw I'd been fishing a little over an hour. I tried the Rapala for another half hour, hoping to catch the one allowable oversized speck, but by now I'd evidently fallen out of favor with the deities. I was rigging to try for redfish when my cell phone sounded the *Marines' Hymn.* Tacky, yeah, but Mike had programmed it in for me when he and Megan gave me the phone as a retirement gift. I leaned the spinning rod against the gunnels and grabbed the phone.

"This is Mac."

In the background I heard the ominous music from the movie *Jaws* that signaled the great white's imminent attack. "Stay out of the water!" a muffled voice said.

"Who is this?"

"Stay out of the water!" I heard again, and then *click* as the caller hung up.

I punched up the "Recent Calls" function on my phone. It was a local number. I dialed it and got a busy signal. I opened a beer and waited a few minutes, then redialed. Still busy.

Just some kids with nothing better to do on a Saturday morning, I told myself. They'd heard about me discovering the body and decided to have a little fun at my expense. But how the hell did they get my number? I hadn't given it to anybody but the marina and the campground and the local cops. I couldn't imagine Sara Gillman masterminding such a prank. No, she wasn't the type. Neither were Jerry or Donna Meadows, owners of Gulf Pines Campground. Those two were like the favorite aunt and uncle I never knew, not mischievous practical jokesters.

Who, then?

The phone call had squelched my desire to go after redfish or flounder. I burned a lot of time and fuel cruising aimlessly back and forth along the island, soaking up the warm sun while thinking about the body, Sheriff

Pickron, and Ben Merritt, and trying to put something together that made sense. Maybe I was just getting paranoid. After a while I decided to call it a day and head back to the marina. The question of who had made the call was still bugging me when I secured my boat in the slip at three that afternoon.

I didn't feel like cleaning fish, so I carried my catch to the seafood market next door to Gillman's and left them to be dressed. I walked back to the boat, secured my gear, and washed up at a faucet on the dock.

Inside the store Kate stood behind the counter ringing up a customer's purchases. Sara waved from a nearby clothing bin where she was straightening and refolding shirts. Her friendly smile reaffirmed my belief that she had nothing to do with the strange phone call. I waited until Kate finished her transaction, and then walked over.

She saw me coming and flashed a smile. "Hey, there. You're back early. How'd you do?"

"Got my limit of specks," I said, then before she could offer congratulations, I added, "You busy after work? I'd like to talk."

Kate tilted her head. "Talk?"

"Yeah. Let me buy you a drink, or supper. I'd appreciate it."

She hesitated long enough for me to think I was being deep-sixed. A customer walked up holding a couple of lures and a handful of other tackle. Kate looked past me. "Be right with you, sir."

"Six-thirty, Mac," she said, adding a quick smile. "Meet me here."

I headed for my truck feeling like I was walking on clouds. A date with Kate; poetic. Well, it wasn't really a date, just a spur-of-the-moment request of her time. I'd caught her with her guard down; she'd agreed under pressure because a customer was waiting to be served.

Damn it, sooner or later I was going to have to shake off this negativity my ex had dumped on me. Jill had been dating up a storm for a couple of years, and now, according to the kids, she'd set her sights on some Navy commander. A chopper pilot, no less; an officer and a gentleman. Maybe that's why Bo Pickron bugged me. As for me, I was an over-the-hill ex-grunt whose post-marital love life consisted of picking up a couple of women in bars after I'd gotten drunk enough to muster the courage. This had to stop sometime.

When I got to the truck I knew something was wrong. It was listing to the left. I checked the tires. Sure enough, the left rear was flat. I muttered a few choice words, then stooped down to drop the spare and jack from under the bed.

The flat had just lifted free of the pavement when I noticed a jagged slash in the sidewall. Somebody had knifed the damned thing. I put the spare on, tightened the lug nuts, and tossed the ruined tire into the bed. I climbed into the cab and started the engine. Slashed tire . . . "Stay out of the water." What the hell was going on?

CHAPTER 5

I drove the few blocks inland to Gulf Pines Campground and turned onto the crushed shell road that wound through two acres of tall slash pines. I waved to a couple of my temporary neighbors whose Weber was flaming like a bonfire. I rounded a curve and parked in front of the double-wide mobile home that Jerry and Donna Meadows had gutted and remodeled to serve as campground office and convenience store. Grabbing the package off the seat, I climbed the concrete steps and crossed the deck.

I'd told Jerry and Donna about finding the body the evening it happened. We'd become fast friends almost as soon as I'd paid the first week's rental on my campsite, and I thought they deserved to know before the news got out and rumors started flying. Also, I knew they could be trusted to pass the truth around, sparing me a lot grief from curious neighboring campers.

There were just a few customers milling about the aisles despite the campground being nearly full for the weekend. Donna was sitting behind the counter watching a talk show on the wall-mounted TV while working knitting needles with the ease that comes from years of experience. We exchanged greetings as I walked past stacks of bundled firewood to get a six-pack of Bud from the cooler. On the way back I grabbed a box of saltine crackers from a shelf.

"Where's that old man of yours?"

Donna's fingers kept working as she glanced up. "Hey, Mac. Jerry's gone to Parkersville. We needed a few things from Sam's Club."

"Got a little something for you," I said, placing the beer, crackers, and the neatly wrapped package of fish on the countertop. "Speckled trout fillets."

Donna's eyes lit up as she peered over her glasses. She set the knitting aside and walked over. "Lord, must be five, six pounds here."

"Four and a half," I said. "I thought they'd dress out more. Guess they shrunk some, or the fish house shorted me."

She chuckled. "Thank you kindly, Mac. Jerry does love his fried trout. I'll fix us a mess tonight. Why don't you come eat with us?"

"Thanks, but I've got a hot date. Appreciate the invite, though."

"Well, a rain check then. And put that money away," Donna said as I pulled out my wallet.

I'd just stepped inside my Grey Wolf and turned on the roof A/C to chase out some of the heat when my phone rang. It was Kate.

"We've got a problem, Mac."

I felt my ego deflate. "Let me guess. You're working late."

"I wish it was that simple. The police are here. You need to come to the marina right away."

A hundred things flashed through my mind, then I remembered my flat. "Is this about my tire?"

"Tire?"

"Yeah. When I got back to my truck this afternoon I had a flat. Looks like somebody took a knife to it."

I heard Kate exhale. "No, it's not about any dang tire. Chief Merritt's here. He wants to see you. Now."

I pulled out of the campground wondering what the hell was going on. If this was a police matter, why hadn't they called me personally or stopped by my campsite? They had my number, and it was no secret where I was staying. Was this about the body? If so, why did the local police want to see me instead of the sheriff's department? What the hell had I done to warrant Ben Merritt's immediate attention?

This day was turning out to be one for the books. First the strange call, then the slashed tire, and now the local cops wanted to see me.

What was that saying about the third time being a charm? I felt anything but charmed. Not to mention my date with Kate was probably shot.

When I pulled into the parking lot ten minutes later Chief Merritt was waiting out front leaning against the door of his blue and white cruiser near the store's entrance. I parked a few spaces away and got out. I glanced toward the store and saw Kate staring out the door. I tried to read the look on her face—worry, disappointment, disgust?—I wasn't sure, but I didn't like it.

"We got ourselves a little situation here, McClellan," the chief said, by way of greeting.

What had happened to "call me Mac, and call me Ben?" This couldn't be a good sign. I pointed to my truck. "There's a little situation in the back of my truck. Somebody slashed my tire while I was out fishing today."

"That so? Well, we'll see about that later," he said, with the same hint of a grin I'd noticed in his office yesterday. "Right now we got us some bigger shrimp to boil. Come with me."

The chief stepped onto the sidewalk and lumbered around the side of the store to the wooden walkway leading down to the docks. I followed, by habit keeping a pace behind and to his left, the proper courtesy enlisted personnel showed officers. Damn, it was going to take forever to shake the military out of my system.

When the chief took a right at the bottom of the steps it finally dawned on me that this had something to do with my boat. What, I had no idea. There weren't any fire hydrants or yellow curbs near my slip that I was aware of. And I sure as hell hadn't double-parked.

As we approached slip 14 a young patrolman holding a camera straightened up from the piling he'd been leaning against. "I got the photos, Chief," the tall beanpole said, holding up the camera. He glanced at me. "Is this the perpetrator?"

Merritt glared at the young man. "Take a hike, Owens."

Without a word, Owens took off at a fast clip.

"Damn trainee."

"Perpetrator?" I mumbled, wondering just what the hell I'd perpetrated.

The chief pointed to my boat. "You care to explain that?"

I looked at the boat. Trusting sort that I am, my remaining rods were in their holders. My tackle box and radio were stored under the bow. The outboard and fuel tanks were in place. I'd done a decent of job policing up the trash, no beer cans lying around. Everything seemed in order. "Explain what?"

"This," Merritt said, grunting as he squatted and pointed at my ice chest.

"What? Oh." A plastic baggie was wedged between the cooler and the gunnels, about a third of it sticking out the side. I must've overlooked it while cleaning up. "You're busting me for littering my boat?"

"That's very funny, Mac. Take a closer look."

Mac. Back to the friendly cop. I looked. The baggie was half-filled with what appeared to be rust-colored parsley or some other herb. I reached down to pick it up for closer inspection.

"Don't touch it!" the chief said.

My arm jerked back. "What?"

Merritt shot me a hard look. "It's marijuana. Some anonymous caller tipped us off."

"Marijuana? You sure?" The stuff wasn't even green. I'd never used the wacky weed personally, but from what I knew it was supposed to be greenish, not rusty brown.

Merritt glanced up from his crouch. "Where did you get it, Mac?"

"I *didn't* 'get it,' Ben. I never laid eyes on it before." If he came back with "You can call me Chief Merritt," I swore to myself I'd punch his running lights out.

He grunted again as he struggled to stand. "I want to believe you, Mac, I really do. The truth is, a bale of this stuff was found on the island a few weeks ago right near where you found the corpse. And this isn't your everyday pot we're talking about here. This is Panama Red."

"Panama Red? Never heard of it."

Chief Merritt hitched up his pants and straightened his belt buckle. "Strong stuff. Rare nowadays. Back in the sixties and seventies it was considered the cream of the pot crop. It disappeared about the same time the hippies did, but it's been making a comeback lately."

I'd already heard more than I ever wanted to about Panama Red or any other strain of marijuana. "Thanks for the history lesson, but I'm telling you I don't know anything about this crap. Somebody must've planted it here."

Merritt didn't offer a comment but reached into a back pocket and pulled out a folded gallon-size plastic storage bag. Grabbing a handkerchief from his shirt pocket, the chief bent to a knee and carefully picked up the baggie by a corner. He slipped it into the larger bag and stood up, knees cracking.

"I'll get this fingerprinted," he said, "and we'll have to give this boat a thorough going over, so don't plan on using it for a few days."

The chief could've saved his breath. Between hooking a bloated body and finding a bag of marijuana stashed aboard my boat, I'd lost interest in maritime sports for the time being. I glanced at the evidence he held in his hand. Something caught my attention.

I motioned to the baggie inside the larger bag. "Could I get a closer look at that?"

"Sure." He held it at eye level for me.

"Ben."

"What?"

"That sandwich bag . . . it's the same brand I've been using for my lunch all week."

The next morning I wasn't the least bit surprised when Chief Merritt called to inform me that my fingerprints alone showed up all over the baggie. I was glad I'd persuaded the chief to search through the garbage can where I'd tossed my trash. Patrolman Owens had proudly produced a handful of similar bags I'd accumulated over the past several days. At least I'd managed to plant the idea that someone could've retrieved one of the sandwich baggies and conveniently placed it in my boat along with its new contents. Most likely the anonymous caller.

Speaking of the boat, Ben Merritt was a man of his word. Fish and Wildlife officially impounded it and gave it more than a thorough going over. The good folks at Gillman's Marina were none too pleased with the stripped-down version that was returned to them a few days later. Somebody's insurance, probably mine, would eventually cover the cost of refurbishing, but it was one less rental from their fleet until the work was completed. At least my gear had been returned in full.

As for the matter of my slashed tire, Chief Merritt practically laughed in my face. There were no witnesses, so how the hell did I intend to prove the tire was slashed? "Hope you bought road hazard coverage, Mac," was how he chalked up it up.

With the heartfelt concern the chief showed for my ruined tire, I wasn't about to have him look into the "Jaws" phone call I'd received while fishing The Stumps. Instead, I decided to call the number again; after several rings a woman answered.

"Hello, I'm trying to reach Decker's Auto and Tires," I said, remembering the name of the business in Parkersville where I'd earlier bought a tire pressure gauge and a can of car wax.

"Sorry, hon, you got the wrong number. This is Jim and Jan's Laundromat in St. George."

I apologized and hung up. A couple of hours later I drove to Jim and Jan's. It was located next to the hardware store where I'd bought a tube of silicone caulk to seal a leaking vent on my trailer the week before. I walked in and glanced around. Coin-operated washers and dryers lined the chalky yellow concrete block walls. A few women sat on benches reading magazines or talking on cell phones while waiting for their clothes to finish washing or drying. An older couple stood at one of several long tables, folding clothes and stacking them in a laundry basket. There was no sign of an attendant, and the only telephone I saw was a pay phone tucked away in a corner of the building near the restrooms.

Back inside my truck, I had a decent view of the pay phone through the laundry's dusty plate glass window. I flipped open my cell phone and checked the number again, then dialed it. It rang a couple of times before a portly woman put down a magazine and ambled toward the phone. I waited until she picked up and offered a listless "Hello," then clicked off. Mystery solved, at least as to where the call had come from.

For a while after the marijuana incident I wasn't the most popular person around Gillman's Marina. I'd brought the business some unwelcome publicity, thanks in large part to an overeager stringer writing for the local newspaper to help pay his way through Parkersville Community College. His embellished article stopped just short of portraying the marina as a front for drug trafficking, and me as a major dealer. I wondered if the kid who wrote it was studying pre-law. The Gillmans were furious, and I heard some loose talk of a libel suit. Sweet Sara wasn't her usual chipper self when I was around either, and even Kate seemed to be turning a cold shoulder my way.

To his credit, Ben Merritt seemed to have bought my version of things or at least given me the benefit of the doubt. I hadn't been charged with any crime, but I *was* informed in no uncertain terms not to leave the area until things were cleared up to his satisfaction. In the course of a few days I'd gone from vacationing fisherman to criminal suspect, with warnings from both the county and city cops not to leave Dodge.

When the fishing bug bit again, Gary Gillman was hesitant to rent another boat to me. But after a week, when he saw I wasn't fleeing the area and was willing to pay two weeks' cash up front, he agreed. I even got my old slip back, since it was no longer a notorious crime scene.

Meanwhile, a sample of the Panama Red had been sent to the Florida Department of Law Enforcement crime lab in Tallahassee to be tested for genetic compatibility with the bale that had washed ashore on Five-Mile Island. I had no doubt it would match. With everything that had happened, I was convinced somebody was running drugs into the St. George Bay area. The body I'd found was probably involved in some way.

And someone was trying real hard to point a finger at me.

CHAPTER 6

A week and a half had passed since I'd found the body, and things seemed to be inching back to normal. I was no longer considered a leper around Gillman's. Sara was back to being her cheery self, and even Kate showed signs of thawing. At least she was smiling and speaking to me again. So when I returned from fishing late Monday afternoon, the somber mood I found inside the marina store caught me off guard.

It was nearing closing time. A young couple with a toddler in tow strolled down the souvenir aisle. Sara, who worked most afternoons since school had let out, wasn't around, and it didn't take long to notice something was troubling Kate. There was no smile or greeting when I walked in, and as I approached the counter I could see she'd been crying. I knew the symptoms all too well. Without a doubt, bad news was in the air.

I waited until she'd finished a transaction with the last customer in line. "What's up?" I said, searching her reddened eyes.

Kate sniffed. "I can't talk now, Mac. I close in ten minutes. Can you wait?"

"Sure, I'll meet you outside. You okay?"

She nodded and sniffled again. "See you in a few minutes."

I sat in my truck and watched the young family exit the store. A few minutes later the lights dimmed. Kate pushed open the door, holding something under an arm as she fumbled with her keys. I climbed out and walked over. She handed me a six-pack of Bud to free up her hands, then locked the door, giving a final tug to make certain it was secured.

45

She turned and flung her arms around my shoulders, buried her face against my chest and burst out crying. "Oh, Mac, it's Maddie!" she choked out between sobs.

I wrapped my free arm around Kate's back, half ashamed of the stirrings I felt as she sought comfort. Who the hell was Maddie? I was certain Kate had never mentioned anyone by that name before. "What happened to Maddie?"

Kate took some deep breaths to regain her composure. "The body you found. They identified her this morning. It's Maddie Harper."

When Kate had calmed down enough, we crossed the highway and strolled along the beach, sipping beer and listening to the calming surf while she filled me in about Maddie Harper and the day's events.

Just before noon, Gary Gillman had received a call from an acquaintance at the sheriff's department. Using dental records, the body I'd found had been positively identified as that of twenty-year-old Madison Lynn Harper. Official cause of death had not been released.

"Maddie" Harper had worked at Gillman's Marina every summer from middle school until she left for college at Florida State last August. At age six Maddie had been involved in a horrific traffic accident that claimed the lives of her parents, Nelson and Mynta, and older brother, Nelson Junior. It had taken a year to fully recover from her injuries. Forced to begin school late, Maddie and Sara Gillman had become close friends—almost like sisters, by Kate's account—despite two-plus years' difference in age.

"With both her parents gone, Maddie's aunt and uncle took her in," Kate said, as we retreated a few feet up the beach to escape the foam of an incoming wave.

I stopped in my tracks. Harper, the real estate business. "Was Maddie kin to George Harper, the mayor?"

Kate took a sip from her beer and nodded. "From what I understand, Maddie's father named his brother as executor in his will. It was a no-brainer, really. The Harper brothers married twin sisters. George and Marilyn were to look after the real estate business and raise the children until they turned twenty-one. Of course, only Maddie survived the wreck."

Kate was tearing up again. I hated to bring up a sore subject, espe-cially when Kate was hurting, but it was eating at me. "That day . . . Dave Reilly mentioned something about Bo Pickron being kin to the mayor?"

Kate wiped her eyes and sniffled. "They're brothers-in-law. Mad-die's mom and aunt are Bo's older sisters."

So, the poor dead girl I'd found was Bo Pickron's niece. I tried to let that news sink in as Kate and I walked on in silence. As much as he rubbed me raw, at that moment I allowed myself a twinge of sympathy for the sheriff. There he was, investigating a floater, observing as the Fish and Wildlife team recovered and placed the bloated remains in a body bag, all the while having no idea he was watching them bag up his own flesh and blood.

We stopped at the city pier and watched the sun paint the horizon red and gold as the gulf swallowed the bright-orange ball. I placed our empty bottles in the carton and opened fresh beers for both of us.

"There's something I just don't get," I said, dropping the caps into my pocket and taking a swig. "Where had Maddie been? Why hadn't she been reported missing? She obviously hadn't been in contact with friends or family for a while."

Kate leaned against a piling, took a deep breath, and let it out slowly. "It's complicated. About a month ago Maddie and her boyfriend eloped. The Harpers never liked Brett, even though he and Maddie had been dating since Maddie was a freshman."

"Then why did they allow her to see the guy?"

Kate sighed and gazed past me for a moment. "Young love, Mac," she said, looking into my eyes again. "You have a daughter, you should know. After a while the Harpers realized that Maddie and Brett were determined to see each other even if it was behind their backs. So, they tolerated the relationship."

I didn't offer a reply but I saw Kate's point. In my opinion, none of the young men Megan had dated ever seemed quite good enough for her.

"The Harpers never cared much for Brett's family either, for that matter," Kate said, "which is odd if you ask me. George and Marilyn Harper have never shied away from money, and the Barfields have made a fortune in commercial fishing."

"The Barfields?" I recognized the name. They operated a fleet of fishing and shrimping boats near the causeway at the east end of St. George.

Kate nodded and took another sip. "Anyway, Maddie got pregnant." She must've read the surprise in my eyes. "Sara told me. I already mentioned they were like sisters.

"Maddie and Brett knew the Harpers would be furious and would never approve of their getting married, even with a baby coming, so they decided to elope. They left notes for both families and drove to Georgia to get married. They planned to spend a couple of weeks backpacking the Appalachian Trail. Being the real outdoors type, they thought the time away in a secluded place would give the Harpers a chance to cool down and maybe accept things."

Kate paused to sip her beer. "Sara swore me to secrecy. Maddie promised Sara she would call when she could. When Sara and the Barfields hadn't heard from Maddie or Brett after a while, they chalked it up to poor cell reception along the trail, or the fact they were having too much fun as honeymooning newlyweds."

"But what about the Harpers?" I said as we turned back. "Did they try to set the law on their trail, find out where they were or anything?"

"I don't know, Mac, but what *could* they do, legally? Maddie and Brett were both of legal age. I did learn the Harpers gave Maddie's dental records to the sheriff's office a few days after you discovered the body. It was just a long shot, but they hadn't heard from her in so long."

"Learned from who, Bo Pickron?"

"Yes. Does that bother you?"

"No." It was a lie. I finished the beer and opened another, my mind swirling. The newlyweds obviously hadn't made it to the Appalachian Trail, or if they had, it was one hell of a short hike. How did they wind up back in this area without anyone knowing about it? And why hadn't Maddie or Brett contacted friends or family?

Maddie, especially. A newlywed with a baby on the way. Wasn't that usually a time of joy for young women; a time for wedding planning and baby showers, and sharing with close friends the fantasies of happily-ever-after married life?

And what about Brett Barfield? Just where the hell was he? No word from him or Maddie in a month, and now his lovely young bride turns up, not refreshed and invigorated from honeymooning on the Appalachian Trail, but as crab bait in a tangle of sea grass just a few miles from his family's business.

The more I thought about it, the more I realized that maybe the Harpers had good cause to dislike the young man after all.

The medical examiner's office released the remains of Madison Lynn Harper to the family on Wednesday. The funeral was scheduled for two p.m. Friday at St. George United Methodist Church. When Kate asked me to escort her to the service, I agreed. I knew she could use the support; Kate and Maddie had grown close during the few summers they worked together at Gillman's. I also felt obligated to attend because I was the person who had found poor Maddie's body. I'd come to hate memorial services, but I knew in this case it was the right thing to do.

On Friday afternoon I followed the directions Kate had given me, turning left onto Seventh Street in front of The Green Parrot Bar and Grill. I counted six blocks, then began checking house numbers on the right and pulled into Kate's driveway. It was a modest one-story stucco cottage, painted aqua with darker blue trim. The lawn was freshly mowed, and a flower garden fronted the porch on both sides of the steps. I straightened my fake necktie and climbed out of the truck just as the front door opened and Kate stepped onto the porch. She waved and closed the door.

"You look very nice," I said, admiring the knee-length navy dress as I held open the passenger-side door. It was the first time I'd seen her wearing anything other than a Gillman's polo with jeans or shorts.

Kate managed a smile. "Thanks, Mac, you look good yourself, all dressed up," she said, sliding onto the seat and straightening her hem.

The church sanctuary was packed. There were few dry eyes as we walked past row after row of mourners come to pay their last respects. A pew had been reserved near the front for the employees of Gillman's Marina. Sara sat between her parents, dabbing now and then at red, swollen eyes with a handkerchief she clutched in her lap. Kate walked past the pew to the closed casket that was surrounded and covered with dozens of beautiful floral arrangements. I followed and stood at parade-rest with head bowed. Kate sniffled and reached out to touch a large framed photo of Maddie Harper resting atop the ornate casket.

Big, tough Marine that I'd always considered myself to be, my gut wrenched and my throat tightened when I gazed at the photograph. Until that moment I hadn't allowed myself to consider the body I'd found to be anything other than a non-person, a lump of bloated flesh, faceless, nameless, like the mujahedeen we'd fought to the death in the streets and buildings of Fallujah. But Madison Lynn Harper had been much more than that. She'd been a beautiful young woman, vibrant, alive, with what should have been a long, wonderful life ahead of her. But Maddie had been cheated out of all that, her life and future snatched away in a moment of terror I could only imagine.

My Megan's face flashed through my mind as I blinked back a tear. What would I feel if it were her lying dead in that casket, gone forever before she'd had the chance to really experience all life had to offer? I couldn't imagine. The thought scared and sickened me. I glanced at Maddie Harper's image once more as Kate turned to go.

I uttered a silent prayer, and then swore I wouldn't rest until I found out what, or who, was responsible for Maddie's death.

CHAPTER 7

The phone call from Sheriff Bo Pickron early Monday morning took me by surprise. Could I stop by his office sometime soon? he'd asked. There was something he wanted to discuss with me. I agreed to meet him at two that afternoon.

I'd spoken to Pickron after Maddie's funeral to offer my condolences. He was visibly upset, shaking my hand and managing to choke out a weak "thank you." It wasn't what I'd expected from the growling hulk I'd butted heads with at the Trade Winds the day I'd discovered the body. Not even the comforting hug Kate gave Bo could dispel the pang of sympathy I felt for the guy at the moment.

George and Marilyn Harper were standing next to Pickron in the family receiving line. Marilyn Harper could barely stand. She leaned heavily against her brother (not her husband, I noted). Dark circles beneath reddened eyes trumpeted pain from her death mask of a face. When I said how sorry I was for her loss, she'd blubbered something I couldn't make out, her breath reeking of alcohol. Maddie's Aunt Marilyn was soaked with grief, head to foot.

By contrast, if there was anything to be read from George Harper's expression, it was a hefty dose of stoicism. There was no sign of grief or pain in his eyes or the lines of his face, and he acknowledged my words of condolence with a mere nod. Maybe he was simply the strong, silent type. Maybe.

A somber Sheriff Pickron was standing behind his desk when I walked into his office. He extended his arm across the big oak desk, and we shook hands. He motioned to a nearby chair. "Have a seat."

When we were both seated he slid open a desk drawer. "I've got something for you," he said and slid my pocketknife across the desk.

I slipped the knife into my shorts pocket, fighting the urge to smart-off about him being absolutely certain it wasn't the murder weapon. The lingering image of Maddie's photo on the casket stopped me. "Thanks. What about my rod and reel?"

"No can do. If this turns out to be murder and goes to trial, we'll need it for evidence."

Truth is, I was somewhat relieved to hear it. I wanted no part of that combo or lure after what I'd caught.

The sheriff leaned forward, resting both arms on the desk. "Listen, McClellan, I think we got off on the wrong foot that day you . . ." He turned his head and stared out the window to his left. "I had no idea it might be my niece. She was supposed to be somewhere up in the Georgia or North Carolina mountains."

"I already told you how sorry I am about Maddie," I said. "I have a daughter and son near her age." I knew he hadn't called me to his office just to return my knife, or for a social visit, but I wasn't going to push him for a reason.

"There was no water in Maddie's lungs," Pickron blurted out. "She died from blunt force trauma to the head, or a broken neck. Either one would've been fatal. It'll be on the news this evening, so that's on the record." He stared hard, like he was trying to see through me. "What I'm about to tell you is strictly off the record. Not a word to anyone. Agreed?"

"You've got my word," I said, wondering why the hell he would tell me anything in confidence.

"I'm telling you this because I think somebody is trying to set you up. That bag of pot they found on your boat? A month ago a bale of it washed up on the island not far from where you found Maddie."

It hardly made sense for the sheriff to swear me to silence over a pot bale washing ashore, since the incident had made the local news before I arrived in the area. "Chief Merritt already told me that. He called it Panama Red, said it was unusual stuff. Is that what I'm supposed to keep quiet about?"

Pickron frowned and shook his head. "Think about it a minute,

McClellan," he said, sounding more like the old Bo. "You show up in St. George, find a body near where a hundred thousand dollars' worth of pot washed up, then somebody plants a bag of the same crap on your boat. If I'm reading this right, you're being targeted for whatever reason, and that might be some help to me down the line."

And if *I* was reading this right, Bo Pickron had an idea I might make good bait for whoever was running drugs into the area. I had no idea how Maddie had wound up behind the Trade Winds Lodge when she was supposed to be honeymooning six hundred miles away in the mountains, but I still wasn't totally convinced there was a link between her death and the Panama Red.

I took a deep breath and let it out. "So, you're telling me you think there's a connection between your niece's death and the marijuana?"

Pickron leaned back in his chair and pressed his fingertips together, forming a steeple. "I told you what the autopsy showed."

I nodded. "But it could've been a boating accident. Maybe she and Brett were hot-rodding and ran into a piling or something; Maddie got thrown out and hit her head."

"There's only one problem with that," Pickron said, opening the drawer again and shoving some papers my way. "That's the autopsy report. Check the bottom of page three."

I did as the sheriff instructed. I read it again, then looked up and met Bo Pickron's eyes.

"Limestone?"

By the time I left the sheriff's office I'd learned a few things. For starters, Sheriff Bocephus Pickron and Chief Benjamin Merritt didn't care much for each other. Whether their beef was a personal or professional matter I had no clue, but I intended to find out. Because the body was found outside the city of St. George's jurisdiction, Pickron had chosen not to share with Merritt or the media the fact that traces of limestone rock were imbedded in Maddie's scalp where her skull was bashed in.

Madison Lynn Harper was indeed pregnant, somewhere near the end of the first trimester, according to the report. That backed up Sara Gillman's story of why Maddie and Brett decided to elope. There were also traces of tetrahydrocannabinol—THC—found in Maddie's hair and fatty tissue samples, which showed she had used marijuana in the not-too-distant past. Not a wise thing for an expectant mother, but the drug residue could have pre-dated Maddie's pregnancy.

Regarding Maddie's death, Brett Barfield was top dog among Pickron's suspects. Due to the corpse's deteriorated condition, the coroner was unable to determine whether the death was accidental or had resulted from foul play, but Pickron was absolutely convinced Brett Barfield was responsible. An all-points bulletin had been issued throughout the Southeast with a detailed description of the suspect and the vehicle he'd been driving when he and Maddie left the area.

The plot thickened. Shortly after the alleged elopement, Brett's father, Clayton Barfield, had called the sheriff to report that Brett's personal 18-foot runabout was missing. Mr. Barfield believed his son had been working on it in one of the repair buildings, but when he looked for the boat, it was gone.

What possible purpose would Brett and Maddie have had for a boat if they were hiking the Appalachian Trail? Could someone have stolen Brett's runabout to make it look like he and Maddie had met with an unfortunate accident while boating in the bay?

There was yet another reason why the sheriff had less than a glowing opinion of young Barfield. While still in his teens, Brett had been busted twice by the St. George Police Department for possession of marijuana. Neither charge had stuck. The Barfield family had a slick lawyer from Tallahassee and, apparently, someone with important connections in the hierarchy of Palmetto County politics. One charge had been dropped completely, the other, much more serious involving enough pot for distribution, was reduced to a misdemeanor. But the closest Brett Barfield had come to serving hard time was picking up trash along local roadways for a few weekends.

The sheriff had one other surprise in store for me: "I'd like to deputize you, McClellan."

My jaw dropped.

"With our budget, I'm a little short-handed and could use your help. I've checked your military files. Your fitness reports say you were a top-notch Marine. Good combat record, so you know how to handle yourself. If my niece's death is somehow linked to drugs like I believe it is, well, let's just say those boys don't fool around. I'll be up front with you; it could get dangerous."

Pickron stood and leaned toward me, both meaty hands on the desktop. "You'd be working undercover and reporting only to me. Sniff around, see what you can find out about Barfield, how my niece wound up in the bay with her skull cracked by limestone rock; how the Panama Red might be connected. What do you say?"

I thought it over a minute. "Why the deputizing bit? Can't I just do some snooping on my own?"

Pickron grunted. "Have it your way. This is still a free country, but if you run into any trouble, you'll be on your own. My way, you got the law on your side. How about it?"

As I got up to leave, I remembered Kate's words about steering clear of Bo Pickron. "I'll think about it."

My gut instinct told me the sheriff was on the up and up, and I tended to trust my gut; it had served me well in Kuwait and Iraq. During our meeting there'd been no patronizing, no "call me Bo, call me Mac" bull hockey. His niece was dead; Brett Barfield was missing, probably on the lam. And Pickron was convinced there was a connection between Maddie's death, Barfield, and the Panama Red that washed up on Five-Mile Island and found its way aboard my rental boat.

Deputy McClellan—it had a nice ring to it. Not quite the weight First Sergeant McClellan carried, but deep down I think I missed the rush that combat brought. This undercover gig might be a nice change of pace from fishing. Still, there was the advice Kate had offered about Pickron the day I discovered the body. What had happened, or what did she know, to tell me to steer clear of him? I needed to know that before I made a decision one way or the other.

I'd already decided on one thing: to become a legal resident of Florida. It would be a requirement if I chose to be deputized, but that wasn't my main reason. I genuinely liked the area and most of the people I'd met, Bo Pickron and Ben Merritt being the exceptions. I figured I could find whatever I was looking to do with my life here as well as anywhere. If I had a change of heart later, I could always hitch up my trailer and move on.

And I won't deny that Kate played a big part in my decision.

That evening I mentioned my intentions to Jerry and Donna Meadows. They were tickled to hear the news. I signed a six-month lease for site 44. It was not only a much better rate, but the lease would help prove my residency. I already had a post office box rented in St. George that would help, too. In the next day or so I'd apply for a Florida driver's license. That should do it.

Now, there was the matter of Kate Bell.

CHAPTER 8

I spent Tuesday morning changing the oil in my truck and thinking over Bo Pickron's offer to deputize me to work undercover for him. The fact that the arrangement would strictly be between the two of us bothered me some. Could I trust him to cover my back if the shit hit the fan, or would he leave my ass hanging out to dry?

Last evening I'd called Kate and learned she worked only half a day Tuesday. I'd been itching to do a little sightseeing to see what the area had to offer besides great fishing, and Kate suggested a day trip to Wakulla Springs State Park that afternoon after she got off work.

"It's a breathtaking place," Kate said, assuming the role of travel agent. "Wakulla Springs is one of the largest and deepest freshwater springs in the entire world. Divers have explored and mapped out hundreds of miles of underwater passages, and it's an archeologist's dream."

"Just how much stock do you own in the place?"

"Very funny, Mac. You'll love it. Besides, they have a great restaurant."

"I knew there had to be a catch in there somewhere."

I pulled into Kate's driveway a little after one. She came bounding down the steps wearing a pair of white shorts and a green button-up blouse with the tail knotted at the midriff, leaving enough skin exposed to immediately cause a stir in my nether regions. Her auburn ponytail was threaded through the back of a matching white ball cap sporting a blue marlin logo.

"Phew, is it just me, or is it hot in here?" I said, pretending to wipe my brow as Kate slid onto the seat next to me.

"It *is* warm today," she said, buckling her seat belt without picking up on my joke, "but just wait till summer really gets here."

Wakulla Springs was a little over an hour's drive from St. George. We headed east on Highway 98, enjoying the beach scenery and each other's company. We drove through Apalachicola, home to what the locals, along with many others far and wide, call the best oysters in the world. Once a sleepy fishing village, the downtown area is fast becoming a popular artists' colony and weekend shopping destination for southern Alabama, Georgia, and Panhandle residents. I'd spent a couple of days there before moving on to St. George.

At the eastern end of town we passed the Gibson Inn, a large, early-twentieth-century three-story wooden structure with wrap-around porches and topped by a cupola. I'd visited their bar at happy hour one evening, and the place was hopping.

"The Gibson is haunted, you know," Kate said, turning in the seat to catch a better glimpse as we drove by.

I snickered.

"It's true, Mac. The ghosts of an old sea captain and a young woman roam around the place. They've been seen by the staff and so many guests that there's no way they could all be making it up."

I laughed. "Yeah, well they've got a great bar in there, too. I never noticed any spooks when I was there, but I'd bet my money that it's mostly spirits conjuring up the spirits."

We crossed the John Gorrie Bridge into Eastpoint, and several miles later we turned north onto Highway 319. I couldn't know it then, but a couple of weeks later I'd be traveling much this same route on more serious business. A few miles farther on I turned onto Wakulla Springs Road and soon came to the park's entrance.

I paid the attendant the six-dollar daily fee, handed Kate the park map, and followed her instructions to the Waterfront Visitor's Center. After finding a parking spot that offered some shade, we hurried across the lot to the ticket window. I shelled out another sixteen bucks for our River Cruise tickets, then we strolled about the grounds to stretch our legs while waiting for the three-thirty cruise.

At three-thirty sharp we boarded the tour boat, a thirty-foot rectangular vessel with open sides for good viewing and a top to provide shade and keep the rain off. Our guide, a young state park employee with longish blond hair and a matching mustache, gave us the official spiel as we glided over the main spring for a moment, which due to recent rainfall was a bit murky instead of the crystal-clear aqua Kate had bragged about.

According to our guide, the bones of mastodons, saber-toothed tigers, and other extinct animals still lay at the bottom of the spring where they had rested since the last Ice Age. We turned downriver, and before long scores of alligators came into view, some sunning on the banks or logs, others watching us drift by with only their eyes and snouts visible above the water.

One curious eight-footer approached the boat way too close for my comfort. Kate leaned over me and snapped photos while I moved my arm away from the rail. No free meals at my expense. And I didn't object when she asked to switch places.

Our guide pointed out a pair of ospreys nesting in the top of a giant cypress, brilliant purple gallinules, the rare limpkin, and other feathered inhabitants of southern swampland swimming or wading in the shallows along the banks. The guide really grabbed my interest when he mentioned that several of the early Tarzan movies starring Johnny Weissmuller had been filmed here, as well as the cult classic *Creature from the Black Lagoon*, one of my all-time favorite flicks as a kid. He even pointed out the huge tree where Tarzan stood beating his chest while belting out his famous "Aaaaeeeeeaaaah!"

I hadn't felt so relaxed in a long time and was sorry to see the tour end. Back ashore after our hour-long, three-mile wilderness adventure, Kate and I visited the rest rooms and then headed for the restaurant for an early dinner before returning to St. George.

Inside the lobby we stopped to pay our respects to Old Joe, a huge stuffed alligator estimated to have been around two hundred years old. Despite his fierce appearance, Old Joe was a docile fixture around the springs before someone murdered the poor beast back in the mid-1960s.

The Ball Room Restaurant, named for the original owner/developer of the Wakulla Springs resort, financier Edward Ball, wasn't anything fancy, but it was comfortable with an old-timey atmosphere about it. A hostess showed us to a table with a view overlooking the springs through huge arched windows. A few minutes later a cute waitress in her teens arrived with menus. She took our drink orders and then disappeared to give us time to select from the dinner fare.

So far, for the entire pleasant afternoon Kate and I had avoided any mention of Maddie Harper or the case I felt myself being drawn into. Finally, after our platters of fried chicken and fried green tomatoes arrived and I'd ordered a third round of drinks, I worked up enough nerve to get down to business.

"I talked to Bo Pickron yesterday. I can't tell you exactly why right now, but I need to know why you warned me to steer clear of him."

Kate pursed her lips and looked away. She took a sip of wine and glanced at me from the corner of her eye. "It wasn't a warning, Mac, it was advice."

"You said he could be trouble."

Her lips tightened even more. She hesitated a few seconds, then turned and stared straight into my eyes. "Okay. I wouldn't let him get into my pants, and he took offense."

That wasn't exactly what I'd expected to hear, but what the hell could that have to do with me? No way could you convince me that Bo Pickron was wired AC/DC. Kate must have read my mind. Her eyes widened, and then she laughed and placed a hand on my arm.

"No, that's not what I meant," she said, stifling another giggle. "Bo tends to get a little rough if he doesn't get his way, or if somebody crosses him."

Now I was pissed. "He hit you?" I'd kill the bastard.

"No, nothing like that," Kate said. "Let's just say he got a little too dang grabby and hard of hearing until I set him straight. Later on, I learned he has a reputation of roughing people up, some on the job, some not, if you get my drift."

So, Bo Pickron was a self-centered chauvinistic jock, not averse to using strong-arm tactics to get his way. Some fine boss he would make. At least Kate had had the good sense to drop him like hot coals when he'd tried to force his charming ways on her. I admired the lady even more now. I placed my hand over hers. "Thanks for being honest with me."

By Thursday I had my Florida driver's license and plates for my truck and trailer. I was now a legal resident of Palmetto County, Florida. Friday morning I drove back to Parkersville for a little shopping excursion. I'd seen several ads for Redmond's Sporting Goods in the newspaper. If the sheriff was correct about somebody targeting me, I figured I'd better have something other than my fists for protection, deputy or not. I was a decent shot with a pistol, but with a shotgun I was hell on wheels. The combat in Fallujah had mostly been up close and personal, and the pump scattergun I carried while serving as company gunnery sergeant had served me well.

After filling out a ton of paperwork I walked out of Redmond's with a Maverick Model 88 twelve-gauge pump. With a twenty-inch barrel and synthetic stock, it's lightweight but packs plenty of wallop— eight rounds of double-ought buckshot worth. I also picked up six boxes of shells. If thirty rounds of double-ought weren't enough for whatever trouble I might run into, odds were I wasn't going to walk away from it anyway.

I still hadn't made up my mind about working undercover for Bo Pickron. No doubt he could be a royal prick, but Maddie Harper was dead, most likely murdered, and I felt I needed to find out why. She'd been Kate's friend and like a big sister to Sara Gillman.

Sheriff Pickron was convinced Brett Barfield was responsible, but I had my doubts about that. By all accounts he and Maddie were crazy in love. According to Sara, when Maddie told Brett she was pregnant he'd agreed they should get married right away. If he somehow *was* involved with her death, what was his motive? And just where the hell was he?

If I was a betting man, I'd give odds he was dead.

That evening I'd just fired up my propane fish cooker for a Cajun shrimp boil when Kate drove up in her Honda CR-V. She parked behind my pickup and slammed the door as she got out. She looked pissed; pissed but sexy in a Gillman's polo and khaki shorts.

"She *lied*, Mac!" Kate's face was flushed and her fists clenched tight. "Ooooh!"

I saw now how Kate was able to set Bo Pickron straight. No way would I want to tangle with the hellcat stomping toward me. She'd been raised with three brothers and could rough and tumble with the best of them. "Who lied?" I said, taking a step back and tightening the grip on my bottle of Bud.

Kate pointed to the beer. "You have another one of those?"

"Yeah, be right back." I hustled inside the trailer and grabbed two Buds from the fridge. Kate was sitting atop the picnic table when I came out, her feet planted on the bench. I twisted off the cap and handed her a beer.

"Now, who lied about what?" I said, taking a seat beside her.

Kate took a long swig and squinted as she swallowed. "Sara! I can't believe she'd lie to me like that. I am so dang ticked at her I could spit nails."

"Okay, what's this about?"

Kate sighed and leaned forward, resting her arms on her bare thighs. "Maddie. Turns out she and Brett weren't going to the mountains after all. They intended to drive up to Donalsonville, Georgia, get married, and then head south to Disney World and the Keys for their honeymoon. Sara knew all about it from the get-go. She lied to cover for them."

"Christ, she must feel like hell." I took a swig and gathered my thoughts. Heading for south Florida and the Keys would explain why the young lovers had taken Brett's boat with them. "Then the notes they left for the Harpers and Barfields were decoys to throw the families off the trail."

Kate nodded. She looked close to tears.

"What about phone calls? Did Maddie ever check in with Sara?"

Kate slugged down a couple of more swallows. "No, and that's why Sara's so upset. She said Maddie planned to call every few days to let her know where they were and what they were up to. But when Maddie never called, Sara got worried. She wanted to tell somebody, but Maddie had made her swear not to tell a soul."

My mind was still churning when Kate drained the last of her beer. I'd never seen her drink so fast. I twisted off the cap and handed her the other. She took a sip and sighed, staring through the pines at nothing in particular.

"Poor Maddie," she said after a minute. "Why on earth are kids so stupid sometimes, Mac? I swear, I could wring Sara's neck."

"For what, being loyal and keeping her word to her best friend?" I finished my beer and set the bottle on the table. "It was probably too late for Maddie before Sara ever expected that first call."

Kate looked at me, her eyes brimming with tears. "I know," she choked out. "I'm just so sorry any of this happened, for Maddie and Sara."

After another beer Kate calmed down enough that I was able to talk her into staying for supper. I spread several layers of newspaper on the picnic table and dumped the basket of Cajun boil on it. We drank beer and feasted on spicy shrimp, potatoes, corn on the cob, and smoked sausage until we were stuffed to the gills. It was dark by the time we finished cleaning up. I grabbed a couple of tumblers and broke out a bottle of single-malt scotch I'd been saving. Kate's company certainly qualified as a special occasion.

We sat outside under a star-filled canopy, sipping scotch and talking long into the night. The full moon finally peeked above the pines and began its slow arc across the sky. Kate got up from her chair and curled up on my lap.

"I'm too dang drunk to drive home tonight, Mac," she said, and kissed me for the first time. "Guess you'll have to let me spend the night."

We kissed again, and then I picked her up and carried her into the trailer.

CHAPTER 9

I eased Kate onto the bed, but she was asleep before her head touched the pillow. I slipped off her shoes and covered her with half the bedspread. For a moment I debated whether to crawl into the bed next to her. I was hungry to hold Kate, but damned if I'd take advantage of her. I cursed my chivalrous Southern upbringing and switched off the lights except for a nightlight beside the refrigerator. Then I grabbed a blanket from a closet to bunk on the pullout sofa for the night. I tossed and turned for an hour or so, listening to Kate's soft breathing. After a while I finally drifted off to sleep.

The next morning I was up before sunrise, but Kate was already gone. I knew she was scheduled to work the weekend. As much as I wanted to see her, I decided to back off for a couple of days. It might've been the booze talking when she wound up in my arms and bed, and I wanted to give her the time and space to sort things out. There was something I needed to check out at the courthouse in Parkersville, but it wouldn't be open until Monday. So, I piddled away the weekend doing some maintenance on my trailer, catching up on some reading, and watching TV.

Monday morning I drove to the courthouse. It was already blazing hot, so I chose a shady spot in the lot across the street to park. Inside the courthouse, I emptied my pockets into a basket and walked through the metal detector manned by a smiling volunteer deputy with silver hair. I grabbed my keys and change and hoofed it down a long hallway that intersected with another. I took a right to the Clerk of the Circuit Court's office. An attractive young woman named Patrice helped me check through the past three months' marriage license applicants. I found what I'd already suspected: Brett Barfield and Madison Lynn

Harper hadn't applied for a marriage license in Palmetto County.

According to Sara Gillman, Maddie and Brett planned to drive to Donalsonville, Georgia, to get married. I drove back to St. George, turned on my laptop, and connected to the Internet. I checked my road atlas, then Googled "Seminole County, GA marriage records" and spent a frustrating hour being bounced from one pay site to another. Finally, I gave up on the web search. I picked up the phone and dialed the Clerk of Court's office in Donalsonville. I wasn't sure if I could access their records over the phone, but to save myself a two-hundred-mile round trip I'd give it a try. It took some sweet talking, but I finally persuaded the lady who took my call to spill the info I was after: no marriage license issued or recorded in Seminole County for Brett and Maddie.

It was beginning to look as if Maddie and Brett never made it to the altar; no license issued or recorded in Florida or Georgia; Maddie Harper found in the bay just a few miles from home; no trace of Brett Barfield in over a month. Nothing added up.

I picked up my phone again, intending to call Kate. It rang before I could punch in Gillman's. I didn't recognize the calling number, but I sure as hell recognized the voice when I answered.

"McClellan, Sheriff Pickron here. You thought any more about our little discussion last week?"

"Yeah, I'm still thinking on it."

There was a short pause. "Well, here's something else you might find interesting. I just got off the phone with the sheriff of White County up in north Georgia."

There was another pause as I tried to unscramble my thoughts.

"You still there, McClellan?"

"Yeah, I'm here." North Georgia? Sara had just spilled the beans to Kate that Maddie and Brett had planned to head for south Florida, not the mountains of north Georgia. "What's this about, Sheriff?"

"They found Brett Barfield's truck outside a little town name of Helen."

I needed to talk to Kate ASAP. I phoned her at work, and we agreed to meet at The Green Parrot that evening at six-thirty. I didn't mention my conversation with Bo Pickron, or that the burned-out hulk of Brett Barfield's Toyota Tundra had been discovered by hikers in a ravine not far from an access point of the Appalachian Trail—the same Appalachian Trail Maddie and Brett planned to backpack, according to Sara's original version of their elopement/honeymoon story. Somebody had some explaining to do.

That evening I arrived at The Green Parrot fifteen minutes early. I found a table next to the rail overlooking the beach and ordered a pitcher of draft Michelob. A young guitarist was singing a Jimmy Buffet tune from the small stage at the deck's far corner when Kate came strolling in. She saw me and walked right over.

"Listen, Mac, about the other night, I—"

"This isn't about that," I said, as she took a seat opposite me. "Besides, nothing happened."

Kate smiled. "I know; always the perfect gentleman. What was your ex-wife thinking?"

If she'd been there, Jill might've made a good argument that I was far from perfect, but I let it drop. "I talked to Bo Pickron again today. Brett Barfield's truck was found in north Georgia, near the Appalachian Trail."

Kate's mouth dropped open, but she didn't speak.

"It should be on the news by late tonight or tomorrow morning. The truck was burned down to the frame."

"Brett?" she managed to squeak out.

"There was no sign of a body in the truck." I grabbed the pitcher and filled her mug. "They're searching the area."

Kate took a sip of beer and frowned. "What's going on between you and Bo?"

I hadn't wanted it to come to this, but given her connection with both Sara and Maddie, I didn't see how I could get far without Kate's help. I glanced around to make sure no one was within earshot. "You can't breathe a word about this to anybody, okay?"

She nodded.

I took a deep breath and let it out. "Pickron wants me to help him look into Maddie's death and Brett's disappearance. He thinks somebody's trying to set me up, probably because I found the body, and that pot was planted on my boat." I didn't tell her that Maddie had most likely died elsewhere and her body dumped in the bay. That fact hadn't been released to the public. And besides, the less Kate was involved, the better.

Kate stared out toward the gulf for a moment, her brow furrowed. "But Sara said they made up the dang story about going to the mountains." She turned back to face me. "I don't get it, Mac."

"Join the crowd," I said, refilling my mug. "How much did you know about Maddie and Brett—as a couple, I mean."

"They were in love, I'm sure of that. Brett would never hurt her."

"Yeah, but what did they do together; where did they like to spend their time, who did they run with?"

Kate sighed and rubbed her brow. "Brett worked a lot, running one of the Barfield boats. When he had time off he and Maddie would go four-wheeling, boating, hanging out on the beach. I told you they were the outdoorsy type. Oh, and they went camping a lot. Brett had this favorite place on some lake up in the national forest. Maddie used to talk about how remote and beautiful it was up there."

I had a swig of beer and took another deep breath. "Don't take this wrong, but do you think Maddie might've been involved with drugs? Marijuana?"

Her eyes narrowed. "No, absolutely not. Why on earth would you even think that?"

"Because Brett was busted for possession. Twice." I didn't mention Maddie's autopsy results.

Kate wasn't aware of Brett Barfield's run-in with the law. It had happened before she moved to St. George, and neither Maddie nor anyone else had ever volunteered the information to her. Sara hadn't confided to anyone but Kate about the ruse of Maddie and Brett honeymooning along the Appalachian Trail. Kate agreed when I asked her to have a heart-to-heart talk with Sara and urge her not to share that information with anyone else for the time being, not even her parents. I also wanted more info on Brett and Maddie's favorite spot in the Apalachicola National Forest. I had a hunch there might just be something there worth looking into. I didn't say that to Kate, but I did ask her to find out all she could about the exact location.

Meanwhile, I decided to take Bo Pickron up on his offer to deputize me. I didn't trust the man any farther than I could throw him, but he seemed willing enough to share information about the case, and if I did run into trouble snooping around, I'd at least have a legal leg to stand on, even if I considered it a shaky one.

The discovery of Brett Barfield's truck in north Georgia was headlined in Tuesday's edition of the *Parkersville Independent*. Brett and Maddie's photos were there too, the same ones the *Independent* had run with the story after her body had been identified. I read the article but found little more info than what Pickron had told me the day before: no body found, a search was in progress in the area the truck was discovered by hikers, Brett was still considered a person of interest in the death of Madison Lynn Harper, yadda yadda yadda.

I poured myself another cup of coffee and started to turn to the sports section when something caught my eye. I glanced at the photos again. Both were your normal senior yearbook poses, but there was something vaguely familiar about Brett's photo that I hadn't noticed earlier. I stared and wracked my brain for a couple of minutes, but I couldn't come up with anything.

After breakfast I called Sheriff Bocephus Pickron, and by two-thirty that afternoon I was a voluntary sworn deputy of temporary tenure. Like Pickron said before, I'd be working undercover on my own and reporting only to him. No badge or identification of any kind to document my status, so I was at Pickron's mercy there. No one else was to know about our little arrangement. I'd already told Kate that Pickron wanted me to help him look into the case, but I hadn't mentioned anything about being deputized, so I hadn't really broken my word to the sheriff. Because I still didn't trust the guy, I decided to keep quiet about the info Sara had spilled to Kate, at least for the time being.

I was on my way back to St. George wondering what my first official move would be when one of Mayor Harper's annoying real estate billboards caught my eye: *Buying? Selling? Renting? See Friendly George for all your real estate needs!*

Friendly George Harper, real estate magnate and mayor of St. George, his wide, gleaming grin, square jaw, and cleft chin plastered all over the county. Then it hit me. I gunned the accelerator and sped home.

I grabbed the newspaper from the recycle stack by the garbage bin and stared at Brett Barfield's photo. The resemblance was remarkable: the same deep-set eyes and square jaw line, but the cleft chin was the ringer. The only mismatch was complexion and hair color: George Harper was blondish and ruddy; Brett Barfield dark-haired and olive. I flipped open my phone and dialed the marina. Kate answered.

"Hey, it's Mac. Do you know if the Barfields and Harpers are related in any way? Cousins, maybe?"

There was a short pause. "No, not that I'm aware of. Why would you want to know that?"

"Just a hunch. I'll tell you about it later."

"I can ask the Gillmans, or Sara when she comes in."

"Yeah, I'd appreciate it if you'd ask Sara when you get the chance. But tell her to keep it between you two, okay?"

After we hung up I looked around and found the phone-book someone had left on my trailer steps a couple of weeks back. I thumbed through the white pages and found the H's. There were about a dozen Harpers listed, and George Herman Harper was among them. I suppose it's only proper for a realtor and the mayor of a city to have a listed home telephone number. George Herman? I dialed the number, wondering if his father or grandfather had been a Babe Ruth fan.

Someone picked up after the fourth ring, and a weary female voice said, "Hello." From what I'd seen and heard at Maddie's funeral, I guessed it was Marilyn Harper.

"Hi, my name's Mac McClellan. Is this the mayor's residence?" I knew it was, but it never hurts to show a bit of courtesy.

"Yes, this is his wife." She sounded a bit slurred. "The mayor's not in at the moment. Did you say your name is McClellan?"

"Yes, ma'am, Mac McClellan. I'm the man who found your niece," I said, never feeling more awkward in my life. "I was wondering if I might have a word with you sometime, at your convenience, of course."

There was a pause, and then the sound of sniffling and clinking glass in the background. "What about, if you don't mind my asking?"

Fair enough. I did some quick thinking. "I'm deeply sorry about Madison, Mrs. Harper. I have a son and daughter around her age, and I can't imagine what you must be going through. I'm hoping to find out what happened to your niece, and why." It was the truth, and if Bo Pickron had a problem with me talking to his sister, we'd have to work it out later.

"Brett Barfield, that *bastard!*" she spit out. "That's who killed my poor Maddie!"

"Yes, ma'am," I said, to placate her, "it looks that way. But we do want to be sure. Could we meet somewhere? I have some questions I'd like to ask you."

There was another pause and tinkling of glass, then a hissed "*Goddammit!*"

"Mrs. Harper?"

"Fine, Mr. McClellan, we'll talk. I have a few questions for you, too. I'm not an early riser. Can you be here, say, two-ish tomorrow?"

"Two's good. Thank you, ma'am."

So, my first official act as a deputized lawman was scheduled. I had a lot of thinking to do about how I would approach Marilyn Harper, and just what I was going to ask her. One thing she'd said during our conversation kept playing over and over in my mind: "Brett Barfield, that *bastard!*"

For some reason, it seemed to fit.

CHAPTER 10

I don't remember how the subject came up, but not long after I'd rented the boat from Gillman's Marina, Lamar told me that the mayor of St. George lived "high on the hog." Lamar wasn't exaggerating. By the time I drove through the stone and wrought iron gateway of the Harper residence north of town, I'd already passed nearly a mile of white wooden fencing fronting the Harper property, the kind you see at topnotch horse ranches. The two-lane asphalt driveway curved through acres of manicured grass shaded by towering pines and sprawling live oaks. I half-expected to find the Tara plantation when I reached the house, and I wasn't far off the mark.

The driveway ended in a wide concrete circle. In the middle of the circle stood a huge fountain with a pair of leaping dolphins spitting water back into the pool. The house wasn't exactly Tara, but throw in some tall columns and a few Southern belles wearing hoop dresses, and you'd be close. I drove halfway around the circle and parked near the edge of the concrete. There was still enough room for a couple of vehicles to pass between my pickup and the fountain.

The two-story red-brick house had plenty of arched windows, a porch that ran the length of the front, and a second-story balcony to match. I started to use the brass knocker on the eight-foot leaded-glass door when I noticed the doorbell. I pushed it and heard the chiming of some fancy tune. I stood there waiting for a butler decked out in a tux. I started to ring a second time when I heard footsteps, and the door opened. It was Marilyn Harper, wearing a beige pantsuit, a string of pearls, and holding a near-empty martini glass.

"Mr. McClellan?" she said, switching the glass to her left hand and extending the other.

"Yes ma'am." I gave her hand a polite squeeze. "Nice to see you again."

She smiled, looking a world better than when I'd seen her at the funeral. She was tall, in her mid- to late-forties, I'd guess, and still an attractive woman despite the recent wear and tear Maddie's death must have caused. "Do come in."

She turned and walked from the foyer into a huge great room. A wide staircase with fancy banisters curved up to the second floor. The vaulted ceiling was a good twenty feet high, with a huge crystal chandelier hanging in the middle. "Would you like a drink, Mr. McClellan?" she said over her shoulder.

"No thanks, and please, call me Mac."

"Well, Mac," she said, as I followed her toward a fancy oak bar that dominated one corner of the room, "I'll have another, if you don't mind."

I hurried past her to the bar where a pitcherful of martinis sat. "No, ma'am, not at all," I said, lifting the pitcher and filling her glass. Call it brownnosing, but it seemed to work.

"Thank you, Mac," she said, crow's-feet showing through her makeup as she smiled. "And you may call me Marilyn, or Mare, if you'd like."

Mare? Why would a woman of her position be nicknamed for a female horse? Then I remembered an actress I'd seen recently on some TV rerun about pioneers, Mare Winningham. I decided Marilyn was informal enough for the mayor's wife.

We moved to the swanky, cream-colored furniture in the great room. I took a seat on the sofa, while Marilyn sat in one of two plush high-backed chairs a few feet across from me. She crossed her legs in a lady-like fashion and sipped her martini. An awkward moment of silence passed. I'd asked for this meeting, so it was up to me to break the ice.

"I was wondering why you and your husband have always disapproved of Brett Barfield," I said, noticing that her free foot began to jiggle when I mentioned the name.

She took a long sip, staring at me over the glass. "And who told you that, might I ask?"

I let out a breath. "Kate Bell. Your niece worked with her at Gillman's Marina."

Marilyn drained her glass. Her foot jiggled faster. "Would you mind?" she said, holding up the glass.

I hurried to refresh her drink. It seemed like I was onto something, and I didn't want to blow the opportunity.

"I've met Kate," Marilyn said as I handed her the drink. "She seems like a nice enough young woman, but she doesn't know what I know about the Barfields. They're nothing but white trailer trash, and that Brett is the worst of the lot."

"Sara Gillman doesn't seem to think so."

"What would that little snitch know?" Her foot was pumping now.

Little snitch? What would cause Marilyn Harper to call Sara that? "Maddie and Sara were best friends. I'd think she'd know a lot."

With that, Marilyn's foot froze. The glare in her eyes was as if someone had suddenly flipped on a hate switch. She uncrossed her legs and stood up. "I don't give a goddamn *what* Kate Bell or Sara Gillman or anyone else says, for that matter!" She practically spit the words. "The Barfields are trash! That woman has had it in for me ever since George broke up with her to date me, and that son of hers was *never* good enough for my Maddie!"

She waved a circle over her head. "You see all this?" she said in a voice loud and nasty enough to peel paint. "It all belongs to Maddie, it's all from *her* money! Before Maddie's parents were killed, the high and mighty Mayor George Harper was nothing but a two-bit car salesman. This is all from blood money, *Maddie's* money, and now my Maddie is gone!"

She burst out crying. I walked over to see if I could calm her down. "I'm sorry, I didn't mean to upset you." I meant it; the poor woman had been through enough.

She sat down before I reached her and held up the glass, then covered her face with both hands and sobbed. I refilled the glass again and handed it to her. She had stopped crying.

"You said on the phone that you had some questions for me," I said.

She slurped down about half the martini and waved her hand. "Never mind," she said. "I think it's best if you left."

"Yes ma'am." I let myself out.

On the way out the gate I punched in Sheriff Pickron's personal cell phone number he'd given me after the deputizing hoopla. "Are you at your office?" I said when he answered. "We need to talk." He was in the vicinity and agreed to meet me at his office in forty-five minutes. I drove through St. George and headed west on Highway 98 toward Parkersville.

I didn't know what had turned Marilyn Harper into a screaming banshee, but whatever it was had to be something important. Hatred that strong didn't sprout from just some social spat or disapproval of a niece's boyfriend. And she didn't seem particularly fond of Friendly George, either. She had leaned on her brother for support at Maddie's funeral, and I figured Bo Pickron must have the answers. Whether he was willing to let me in on them was a different matter.

When I got to the office his attractive young secretary announced my arrival and waved me on to Pickron's office. I walked in and made sure to shut the door behind me, thinking this meeting might turn out to be a little less than cordial. Pickron was sitting on the edge of his desk, arms folded, and didn't look the least bit happy. I'd counted on the fact that Marilyn would most likely call her brother and whine to him about our little visit, and I wasn't wrong.

"Just what the hell were you thinking, talking to my sister that way?" he said, loud enough that the closed door probably didn't offer much privacy, if any.

"Look, you're the one who asked me to check into Maddie's death and Barfield's disappearance. Just how the hell am I supposed to do that if I don't question people who might know something?"

He got up off the desk and stood right in my face, snarling like one of my drill instructors back on Parris Island. "You stay the hell away from my sister!" he said and poked me in the chest with a finger.

I slapped his hand away, and it was all I could do to keep from smashing my fist into his groin, one of the first moves they'd taught us during hand-to-hand training at P.I. The sudden move caught him off guard, and he backed away, eyes blinking. I figured then he wasn't used to people pushing back.

"Now hold on, McClellan," he said after a few seconds. He raised his palms. "You're right. Let's calm down and talk this out."

Bocephus Pickron didn't exactly bare his soul to me, but I did learn a few things before I left his office a half hour later. Maybe the most important bit of info he coughed up was that Madison Lynn Harper would've become a very rich young woman had she lived to see her twenty-first birthday. Her father, Nelson, began dabbling in real estate while still in college, and by his mid-twenties was owner of one of the fastest-growing companies in the Panhandle. Maddie stood to inherit the bulk of several million dollars in stocks, cash, and real estate holdings, plus the Harper house and property she'd grown up in. "Tara" had belonged to Nelson and Mynta Harper, not George and Marilyn.

The way I saw it, because of Maddie's inheritance, Mayor Harper was one big waving red flag, but Pickron didn't think so. "I've known George all my life," he said. "He might be a lot of things, but he's no murderer. He loved my niece like she was his own daughter."

Because of a medical problem Marilyn was unable to have children, and the Harpers had been looking into adoption before the tragic accident landed Maddie in their laps, and them in the midst of Nelson and Mynta's fortune and opulent lifestyle.

One thing George Harper was, the sheriff admitted, was a philanderer who couldn't keep his pants zipped tight. I almost laughed when

Pickron told me that. What's the saying? Brothers-in-law of a feather flock together? Something like that.

George's indiscretions began while he and Marilyn were dating in high school and had continued throughout their twenty-plus years of marriage. I suppose Marilyn put up with George because she'd grown accustomed to the money and the swanky high-society life it provided, and she valued that more than their wedding vows. Also, I had my doubts that she'd always kept to the straight and narrow path of fidelity herself, though I didn't mention that to her brother. There was nothing solid to base my suspicions on; it was just my manly intuition talking again.

As for the Barfields, all Pickron knew, or was willing to spill, was that George Harper and Clayton Barfield had been bitter rivals since they were teenagers and couldn't stand the sight of one another to this day. In high school Clayton Barfield had been an all-conference quarterback, while George Harper saw more action on the bench than on the field.

However, George's father owned a new- and used-car dealership in Parkersville, and the future mayor motored through his high school years driving a fancy set of wheels. He may not have seen a lot of action on the gridiron, but he certainly had in the backseat of his Pontiac GTO with the fairer sex, a few of whom he'd evidently wooed away from Barfield.

Clayton was the product of more modest means, and he spent most of his time while away from school and sports working hard for his family's struggling commercial fishing business. As fate would have it, George took over the auto business when his father died and within a few years ran it into bankruptcy. Clayton, on the other hand, labored long and hard to build Barfield Fisheries into one of the most productive fleets on the Gulf Coast.

I turned east onto Highway 98 and headed home. I hoped to see Kate after work and find out what she'd learned, if anything. Her companionship and a beer would sure be a pleasant change after the day I'd had with Pickron and his sister.

And I knew things weren't going to get any easier when I faced the Barfields.

It was just after four when I pulled into Gillman's parking lot. I picked a space well away from the maniacal mockingbirds but still kept a wary eye peeled as I walked to the store. There were no customers inside that I could see. Kate was behind the counter poring over some figures with an adding machine. Sara was strolling down an aisle trying to look busy. I waved to Sara and walked over to Kate. I was about to ask if she'd meet me for a drink after work when Lamar Randall came striding in through the back entrance.

"How 'bout it, Mac," he said, wiping his greasy hands with a shop rag. "I haven't seen your boat out in a while."

I shot him a grin. "Been slaying the specks so bad I thought I'd give 'em a couple of days to recover."

Lamar chuckled, reached up, and adjusted his eye patch. That's when the tattoo caught my attention. It was one of those crude tattoos with smudgy, faded blue ink that kids often inflict upon themselves or friends in the wayward days of youth. I'd seen it before but never gave it a close look or second thought.

Until now.

Lamar turned his attention to Kate and rested both palms against the edge of the counter, fingers curled up to keep from smearing the glass top. "Would you put two quarts of oil on John Denny's ticket?"

Kate grabbed a notepad and jotted down the info.

"Oh, and I need to talk to Gary about that Yamaha if he gets back before you close up," he added. "It might not be worth rebuilding when you count in all the parts and hours it'll take."

Kate smiled. "I'll leave a note on his desk if he's not back."

"Now," she said, after Lamar said his good-byes and made his exit, "what can I do for you, Mr. McClellan?" Kate's bright eyes gave away her attempt to appear stern and businesslike.

"I was wondering if you might join me at The Green Parrot for drinks and dinner, Miss Bell."

She grinned, the tiny space between her front teeth peeking from between her lips. "How about my place, six-thirty? There's a couple of nice thick rib-eyes waiting to be grilled, if you'll do the honors."

Driving back to the campground, my anticipation of spending an evening with Kate at her invitation was tempered by what I'd seen spelled out in crude lettering across the fingers of Lamar's right hand:

Mare.

CHAPTER 11

That evening Kate greeted me at the door and surprised me with a kiss. I handed her the bottle of merlot I'd bought to go with our steaks, and Kate poured the wine while I fired up her gas grill. We spent a pleasant hour chatting on the deck while my famous grilled potatoes, roasted onions, and the rib-eyes cooked to perfection. By the time we sat down to eat, the aroma had my mouth watering.

I waited until we'd finished our feast before talking business. I grabbed a beer from the fridge and poured Kate another glass of merlot. We carried our drinks back outside to the deck and sat together on the cedar glider.

Sara Gillman had no knowledge of any relationship between the Harpers and Barfields, other than the fact the families didn't get along for some reason. Maddie and Brett had been in love since middle school and, despite their families' differences and Marilyn Harper's objection, had managed to maintain their relationship all those years.

"All I remember about Brett and Maddie's favorite camping spot is that it's near a lake somewhere in the Grand Gator Bay Wilderness Area in the national forest," Kate said. "It's about forty miles from here. Sara went camping with them a couple of times. She remembers they followed a service road for several miles to a dead end. They parked Brett's truck there and used four-wheelers they trailered for a couple of miles and then hiked the rest of the way. It's pretty rugged country from what I've heard. Sara said they waded through waist-high water in a couple of places along the trail, which she didn't care for at all. She's real afraid of snakes."

"Join the crowd," I said, having never been much of a herpetology fan myself. "You think Sara might remember what service road it was if we showed her a map?"

Kate shrugged. "She might, but what's so dang important about finding their camping spot?"

I swigged my beer. "I know you're not going to like this, but I believe Brett was involved with drugs—marijuana in particular."

Kate shook her head. "Uh-uh, Mac, no way."

"I'm not saying Maddie knew anything about it, but think about this: Brett had two prior arrests for possession. I find Maddie's body near where a bale of pot washed ashore, and then somebody plants a bag of the same stuff on my boat and calls the cops. You don't find that to be a little too coincidental?"

Kate took a sip of wine and stared out into the dark. Fireflies blinked on and off across the yard. "It doesn't prove anything," she said after a minute. "I knew Brett well enough to know he wouldn't have done anything to put Maddie in danger."

"Then what about the honeymoon story they concocted and made Sara swear to keep secret?" I took another swallow. "They cook up a story about eloping and hiking on the Appalachian Trail when they're supposedly heading for Disney World and the Keys. Then Maddie's body winds up in the bay and Brett's truck is found in some ravine in north Georgia. What kind of sense does that make? And just where *is* Mr. Do No Harm?"

Kate didn't answer. She went inside and brought back the bottle of merlot and another beer. "You're right. None of it makes any sense," she said, pouring the wine. "I wish it did."

I took a deep breath and let it out. "I'm not supposed to tell anybody this, but I need somebody to cover my back, and you're the only person I can trust right now."

I hesitated. Kate's brow wrinkled as she took another sip of wine. "What?"

"I know for a fact Maddie's body was dumped in the bay. She didn't die there. And don't ask, because I can't tell you anything more about it."

To say Kate looked shocked would be the understatement of the year. She opened her mouth a couple of times, but nothing came out. I hadn't exactly broken my word to the sheriff. I didn't tell Kate the particulars about Maddie's autopsy, only that her body had been moved after her death.

"There's another thing I haven't told you." I tilted the bottle and drained my beer. Kate was all ears. "Brett's runabout went missing a while back. Maddie's body is dumped in the bay. Brett is nowhere to be found. Looks to me like someone wanted it to appear that they both drowned in a boating accident."

Kate closed her eyes for a moment and massaged the bridge of her nose. "Then why did Brett's truck wind up in Georgia? If somebody wanted people to believe he and Maddie drowned in the bay, why on earth move his truck hundreds of miles north of here?"

It was a good question. I wracked my brain for a minute. "Maybe whoever did this was trying to cover both ends of a dead-end trail. They knew Maddie and Brett left letters for their families about eloping and going to the mountains. But somehow they learned the letters were just a smokescreen to cover Maddie and Brett's real intention of heading to south Florida.

"Whatever Brett was planning went wrong. Whatever happened, Maddie got caught up in it, wound up dead, and her body dumped in the bay. Then someone stole Brett's runabout so that if her body ever turned up, it would look like a boating accident."

I opened the other beer and downed a couple of swallows. "Then somebody drove Brett's truck to Georgia, torched it, and pushed it into the ravine to make it look like Brett—or Brett *and* Maddie—had crashed and wandered off injured into the mountain wilderness. Voilà; two scenarios of how they met their fate, both false."

Kate scooted closer, laid her head on my shoulder, and sighed. "I'm more confused than ever."

So was I. There were still a lot of pieces missing from the puzzle I was trying to force together, and maybe those pieces wouldn't fit even if I found them. Brett Barfield might be the key link. Where was he? Had he learned his lesson from the two priors, or had he been up to no good all along?

And what about Lamar? I certainly didn't have him pegged before as being involved in this mess. Marilyn Harper hated the Barfields with a vengeance; that much was obvious. What was the connection between Lamar and Marilyn Pickron Harper, if any?

Could there be more than one "Mare" in a town this size?

I was at the Parkersville Public Library the next morning when they opened the doors at ten sharp. I walked over to the reference librarian's desk and asked the lady where I could find the Parkersville High School yearbooks. I followed her directions and was soon gathering several volumes of the *Panthers' Pride* from the seventies. It was a guess, but I figured the Harpers, Clayton Barfield, and Lamar Randall to be somewhere in their mid-forties to early fifties.

After a couple of dead ends, I found George Harper and Clayton Barfield listed with the sophomore class in one volume and with the juniors the following year, but there was no trace of the Pickron sisters or Lamar Randall in either. I hit pay dirt with the next volume, George and Clayton's senior year. The pretty Pickron sisters, identical twins Marilyn and Mynta, were voted co-sweethearts of the sophomore class. They belonged to several organizations, including the junior varsity cheerleading squad. Lamar was a fellow-member of the sophomore class. I was hoping to find a connection between Lamar and Marilyn, but after a thorough search through the entire volume I came up empty. His mug shot was there in alphabetical order among the other gawky bottom-dwellers, but that was it.

I searched through the next two volumes but failed to turn up any evidence of a romantic link between the future Mrs. George Harper and Lamar Randall. His high school career was unremarkable at best, while Marilyn Pickron and sister Mynta had shined. Maybe Lamar harbored a crush for Marilyn during middle or even grammar school. At least I'd learned that some of the principals in Maddie's case had attended school together for a few years.

I left the library and drove to Redmond's Sporting Goods. I

remembered they carried a fine supply of nautical charts and topographic maps of the Panhandle area. I told the clerk what I was looking for and chose a detailed roadmap of the entire Apalachicola National Forest and a topo map of the Grand Gator Bay Wilderness Area.

"If you're planning on hiking in that area this time of year," the clerk said, "I'd advise you to invest in a good pair of snake boots."

I declined his offer to sell me a two-hundred-dollar pair of boots, hoping my Marine Corps-issue combat boots would suffice. I did buy a machete, thinking it might come in handy sometime during my little trek through the swamps, a bottle of bug juice, and a two-man tent that weighed less than four pounds.

I drove back to St. George and stopped by the marina, hoping to catch Kate in time for her lunch hour. Luck was with me. We walked across the street to a sandwich shop that overlooked the canal. I ordered a couple of grilled grouper sandwiches and iced teas, and we carried them to the outside deck.

I pulled the roadmap of the forest from my cargo pocket and handed it to Kate. "If you get a chance would you show this to Sara when she comes in today?"

Kate wiped her fingers with a napkin and unfolded the map. She nodded. "She should be able to find the road they took from this."

I swallowed a bite of my sandwich and took a swig of tea. "Try not to let anybody see you, especially Lamar."

Her eyebrows arched. "Lamar? Why Lamar?"

"It's just a hunch. I'll tell you about it later. For now, just trust me, okay?"

Back at the marina I asked Kate to help me pick out a decent mask, set of fins, and a snorkel. "What on earth are you planning to do with this?" she said while bagging my purchases.

I grinned. "Nothing, on earth."

That evening Kate called around seven. "Sara recognized the roads they took to get to Grand Gator and the service road that dead-ended where they parked," she said. "I've already highlighted them on your map. She thinks she knows which trail they took with the four-wheelers, but she's not a hundred percent on that."

"Good. Did anybody see you?"

"No. Lamar left early this afternoon. Gary and Linda were in Parkersville for a couple of hours. There were some customers browsing around, but they weren't paying any attention to us."

"Thanks, Kate. What's the marine forecast for tomorrow? I was thinking about taking the boat out."

"It's good; winds out of the southwest less than five, seas one to two feet. Going fishing?"

"Yeah, you could call it that."

CHAPTER 12

I loaded my gear and left the marina just after daylight, headed for The Stumps. It was my gut talking again. I recalled the tale of Brer Rabbit imploring Brer Fox to "please don't throw me in the briar patch." Maybe that was what the call had been about the morning I'd fished The Stumps: "*Stay out of the water.*" Reverse psychology—maybe somebody *wanted* me to explore The Stumps. If so, I intended to find out why.

As much as I liked Lamar Randall and hated my suspicion, I was beginning to think he might somehow be involved in this mess. He'd been the one to suggest I fish the grass flats behind the Trade Winds and then sent me to The Stumps on my next angling excursion where I'd received the strange "Jaws" theme phone call. It seemed too obvious, but after seeing Marilyn Harper's nickname tattooed across his fingers, it finally dawned on me that one-plus-one just might equal two.

I eased back on the throttle and got as close to The Stumps as I dared before shutting off the motor. A few stoic pelicans perched atop silver-gray stumps ignored me as I dropped the anchor and stood near the bow to give the dead forest a quick survey. There was no sign of a fuel slick, but I remembered seeing one the morning I fished here. At the time I didn't pay it much mind; such slicks aren't uncommon around popular fishing spots, especially where an oil/gas mixture might wash into an area like this and coat the dead stumps.

I kicked off my deck shoes and stripped down to my swim trunks, then grabbed my snorkeling gear from the duffle bag. If Brett Barfield's runabout was on the bottom somewhere in The Stumps I intended to find it. The one thing I'd forgotten was a diver-down flag. It was too late to worry about that now. I hoped Dave Reilly or one of his fellow F and W officers wasn't patrolling in the vicinity.

Early in my Corps career I'd spent a tour in a Recon unit. It had been a decade or more since I'd been SCUBA diving, but I remembered enough of my training to do a little snorkeling and free-diving. I spit into the mask and rinsed it, pulled on the fins, and slipped over the gunnels into the warm water. I cleared the snorkel and eased my way into The Stumps.

Visibility was fair to good, and I could make out the murky bottom, which I estimated to be somewhere around fifteen to twenty feet down. The bottom rose toward shore in a gentle incline. The dead forest was a beautiful but eerie sight. Schools of silvery minnows and small fish darted about, and I spied several speckled trout and a couple of redfish lurking among the ghostly stand of trees. A couple of times I thought I might've found what I was looking for, but each time a quick dive showed it to be downed timber instead.

I worked east to west in a zigzag pattern, trying to cover as much of the area as possible. After a while I glanced at my watch. I'd been at it for twenty minutes with no luck, but I pressed on. I was about three-quarters of the way through The Stumps in twelve or fifteen feet of water when I spotted it: a boat, lying on its side wedged between two large trees.

Adrenalin kicked in, and I took a few seconds to calm myself. Taking several deep breaths to oxygenate my lungs, I dove. Halfway down I felt pressure building in my ears; I pinched my nostrils and blew to equalize them. I swam down to the boat and grabbed hold of the gunnels. I looked it over and estimated it to be a seventeen to twenty footer. I pulled myself hand over hand toward the stern; the outboard was a one-fifteen horsepower Mercury. My lungs were beginning to beg, so I headed to the surface.

I pulled off the mask, gasping for air. I took a good look around, but no other boats were in sight. I rested a minute, spit, and rinsed the mask again, and dove for another look.

This time I swam to the bow. The port side had been bashed in, and there was a sizable hole in the hull about three feet back. From what I could see there was no reason to believe that the damage couldn't have been caused by the boat crashing into The Stumps at a fast clip. I maneuvered to where I could see the boat's interior. There was no sign of a trapped body or life jackets or other gear. I pulled up a bench cover and checked the live-well. It was empty. My air running out, I looked for the registration number on the bow, but the numbers were unreadable due to the damage. The starboard side was resting on the bottom, and I tried but couldn't get to it. By now my lungs were screaming, so I surfaced.

Back aboard my boat, I opened a beer and rested for a few minutes. Then I grabbed my cell phone and punched in Bo Pickron's personal number.

"What kind of boat does Brett Barfield own?" I asked when the sheriff answered my call.

"An Angler, eighteen-footer I think. Why?"

"What kind of motor?"

"I'm not sure. Are we playing Twenty Questions, McClellan?"

"You told me Clayton Barfield reported it missing," I said. "I assume you have a record of it."

"Of course I've got a record," he said, his voice rising. "Give me a minute."

Somehow the agitation in Bocephus's voice pleased me. I sat on the bow with my feet dangling in the water, drinking my beer while I waited for the sheriff to shuffle through whatever filing system he kept. The sun felt good on my back.

"McClellan?"

"Go."

"It's an older eighteen-foot Angler with a one-fifteen horsepower Mercury outboard. And I'll ask you again—what's this about?"

I drained my beer before answering. "I'm anchored at The Stumps. Brett Barfield's boat is lying on the bottom."

Pickron told me to get to his office ASAP and not to breathe a word to anyone about what I'd discovered. He'd be waiting for me. I pulled anchor and headed for the mainland. It was a quarter till two when I strolled past his smiling secretary and into his office.

Pickron was sitting at his desk going through a stack of paperwork. "Just what the hell is going on here?" he said, motioning for me to take a seat. "You show up in town and find my niece's body, which we know was placed in the bay *after* she died. Now you conveniently happen across Barfield's missing boat. What gives?"

I leaned forward and shrugged. "Just lucky, I guess. Maybe I ought to start playing the lottery."

The sheriff popped up out of his chair and pointed at me. "Don't screw with me, McClellan! I got a good mind to throw your ass in the slammer."

"On what charge?" I said, resisting the urge to grab his finger and snap it like a stick. "Look, you asked me to look around and see what I could find out. That's exactly what I've been doing. I've got a couple of leads and I'm checking them out."

"How did you know where to find the boat?"

"It was just a hunch, Sheriff, nothing more," I said, deciding against telling him about the phone call I'd received at The Stumps. "I was fishing The Stumps a few weeks ago and noticed an oil slick. I didn't think anything of it at the time, but after you told me Barfield's boat went missing, I got to thinking about it. So I bought some snorkeling gear and went snooping. End of story."

The next morning Fish and Wildlife and the Palmetto County Dive & Rescue team scoured the area in and around The Stumps for several hours. When they finished, a salvage crew attached air bags and brought the boat to the surface and towed it to the mainland, where it was immediately impounded.

That evening the local television channel headlined the story. A sunken pleasure boat, tentatively thought to belong to Brett Aaron Barfield, twenty-one, had been located just off Five-Mile Island in an area popularly known as The Stumps. Speculation was that young Barfield, missing since early May, had perished in a boating accident along with his girlfriend, Madison Lynn Harper, whose body was recovered several weeks prior behind the Trade Winds Lodge.

There was no word about who made the discovery, which was fine with me. I'd taken enough heat when I'd found Maddie's body; I sure as hell didn't need the notoriety that would follow if the public knew I'd also found Brett's boat. I had enough enemies around these parts already.

For the time being, Bo Pickron was treating me as if I had the plague. All I got from him was that Clayton Barfield had positively identified his son's boat late that afternoon and that the boat's numbers matched the Florida registration. If any evidence had been found on the boat that might shed some light on the case, Pickron wasn't in any mood to share it with me or the media. For all intents and purposes the incident was a tragic accident and Brett Barfield was presumed drowned, body not recovered.

A little after seven that night headlights shined through the windows as a vehicle pulled into my campsite. A car door opened and closed. I peeked through the drawn blinds and saw Kate hustling toward the steps. I opened the door before she was close enough to knock.

"Did you see the news?" she said, rushing inside and dropping her purse on the dinette table.

"Hello to you, too," I said.

"Stop it, Mac, this isn't funny. They found Brett's boat this morning."

"Well, actually, I found it yesterday. Dive & Rescue did their thing this morning."

Kate stopped like she'd been frozen in place. "*You* found it? Is that what the snorkeling gear was . . . but how did you know where to look?"

While I grabbed a couple of beers from the fridge, I told her about the phone call I'd received the morning I'd fished The Stumps, and how I'd traced it to the pay phone at Jim and Jan's Laundromat. We sat at the table and I handed Kate a beer. "What do you know about Lamar's family?"

"I met his wife, Debra, at the Gillman's last Christmas party. She drops by the marina now and then. She's a nurse at Parkersville Memorial, works night shifts mostly, I think. Why? You don't believe Lamar's mixed up in this, do you?"

"Kids?" I said, ignoring her question.

Kate sipped her beer. "They have three, two boys in middle school and a daughter in high school. I think Lamar has an older son from a previous marriage, but he doesn't live around here."

"Any around Sara's age?"

Kate nodded. "Tonya goes to school with Sara. They're friends, but not particularly close that I know of. She's a year behind Sara." She pursed her lips. "No more questions until you tell me what this is about."

"Fair enough." I reached across the table and placed a hand on Kate's. "The day I found Maddie's body it was Lamar who suggested I fish behind the Trade Winds. A couple of days later, he suggested I fish The Stumps."

"What does that prove?" Kate said, shifting in her chair. "Both those places are hot spots for speckled trout, and that's what you were after, isn't it? If I remember correctly, you're the one who kept badgering Lamar for suggestions about where to fish. Why on earth would he send you there if he was mixed up with Maddie and Brett?"

"I don't know, maybe reverse psychology." I recounted the story of Brer Rabbit and Brer Fox from the old Disney movie. "I'm not accusing Lamar of anything at this point, but it sure is one hell of a coincidence, don't you think?"

Kate frowned and fidgeted in her chair, but didn't answer.

"And here's something else to chew on," I said. "You ever notice that tattoo he has scrawled on the fingers of his right hand?"

She nodded.

"Did you ever ask him about it, who 'Mare' is?"

"Of course not. Why on earth would I do that? It's none of my dang business."

I took a swig of beer and fought back a belch. "It might be more your business than you think," I said, searching Kate's eyes. "'Mare' is Marilyn Harper."

I called Bo Pickron's cell phone at eight Monday morning and got his voice mail. Guess he didn't like the sound of my ring tone. I hung up without leaving a message and dialed the sheriff's office. His secretary put me on hold, and I waited a good five minutes before Pickron came on the line.

Investigators were still going over the boat, he said, and if they found anything of interest he'd be sure to let me know. I knew a brush-off when I heard one. At least he hadn't un-deputized me, but I wondered just how much backing I could expect from his office if I found myself in a tight spot.

Around nine-thirty I headed east on Highway 98. It was time to pay a visit to Barfield Fisheries. I decided on a cold call instead of giving them advance notice that I was coming. Twenty minutes later I pulled through the open gate of the Barfield business, which was surrounded by an eight-foot chain-link fence topped with barbed wire standoffs. The weather had been dry lately, and my truck raised a cloud of dust as I drove along the crushed shell road. There were several tall metal buildings roughly the same size, all painted a faded aqua with off-white trim. I spotted the office and parked in front.

A cute young lady in her late teens or early twenties was sitting behind a desk talking on the phone as I walked in. She had a shock of curly red hair, and her pale skin was dotted with freckles.

"Uh-huh, uh-huh," she said, jotting some numbers on a slip of yellow paper. "Right, a hundred pounds of thirty-one forties. Yes, sir, they'll be on tomorrow morning's truck."

I glanced around the room while pretty Orphan Annie took care of business. The walls were paneled in cypress. A few serviceable chairs were arranged along one wall with a couple of lamp tables stacked with magazines thrown into the mix. Several species of salt water fish were mounted on the walls, and behind the young lady's desk a beautiful seven- or eight-foot sailfish looked like it would dart away if returned to the water.

"Can I help you, sir," she said, looking up and smiling as she hung up the phone.

"Is Mr. Barfield in?"

"Which Mr. Barfield do you want?"

"Clayton," I said. I'd overlooked the fact that he might have brothers or other kin working in the family business.

She picked up the phone and punched in a number. "Miz Nora, is Mr. Clayton in his office? There's a gentleman here to see him."

She moved the phone from her ear and covered the mouthpiece. "What's your name, sir?"

"Mac McClellan."

The redhead repeated my name to Miz Nora. Her smile faded, and her cheeks lost what little color they'd held before. "Yes, ma'am," she said.

"You can go on back, sir," she said, pointing past her desk to a hallway. "Mr. Barfield's down on the docks right now, but his wife will see you. Third door on the left."

From the redhead's expression, the Barfields were acquainted with my name. I didn't know if that would work for or against me, but I'd sought them out, so there was no turning back now. I walked down the hallway past photos of boats and people and ball teams lining the walls. The door was open, but I knocked on the frame anyway.

"Please, come in," a pleasant voice said.

I did and was met by a striking lady with jet-black hair and flawless olive skin standing beside a large oak desk. She was decked out in a black knee-length skirt, a white blouse that left just a hint of cleavage showing to grab your attention, and a fancy gold necklace riding just above the attention grabber. Filipino and white, I guessed; I'd seen the combo many times on base. Early forties, maybe. Whatever her age or heritage, she was one sweet package.

"I'm Nora Barfield," she said, extending her hand, "Clayton's wife."

"Mac McClellan, pleased to meet you," I said, careful to keep my eyes above the danger zone. I saw now where Brett got his dark coloring.

At her invitation I took a seat near the desk. She sat behind it where I wouldn't be distracted by the shapely calves I'd noticed beneath the skirt at first glimpse. Something told me I'd seen her before. I doubted it was at Maddie's funeral. Given the bad blood between the two families, I couldn't imagine this genteel lady chancing a ruckus by showing up there even if it was to pay last respects to her son's late girlfriend.

"You're the gentleman who found our Maddie," she said, now looking close to tears.

"Yes, ma'am. That was a terrible day."

Her eyes were brimming. "And now they've found my boy's boat. Clay and I had already prepared ourselves, trying to keep busy and all, but I was still hoping . . ." Her voice trailed off, and she dabbed at her eyes with a tissue.

She looked up, still blotting the tears. "You'll have to forgive me, Mr. McClellan. They were so young, so much in love, and . . ."

I waited a second for her to compose herself. "Not at all," I said, feeling my throat tighten. "I've very sorry for your loss." I was, too. I'd had a bellyful of seeing people grieve. Mike and Megan ran through my mind. I tried to shut them out, not knowing how I'd be able to carry on if I ever lost them.

"Well," she said, sniffing. She sat up straight and forced a smile. "What is it you'd like to see my husband about?"

"I hate to bother you at a time like this," I said, wondering if she was purposely acting as a shield for her husband. "After I discovered Miss Harper's body I felt a responsibility to find out what happened to her and your son. I guess it's because I have children myself near their age."

She pulled a fresh tissue from a box on the desk, turned her head, and gently blew her nose. "I'm not sure I follow you."

I cleared my throat and leaned forward in the chair. "Do you happen to know Kate Bell? She worked with Maddie at Gillman's Marina the past few summers."

Mrs. Barfield nodded. "I've met Kate. Brett and Maddie always spoke highly of her."

"And I'm sure you know Sara Gillman."

"Yes, of course. Sara was Maddie's best friend. My son loved her like a sister." She hesitated a moment. "If you don't mind my asking again, why exactly are you here?"

"Mrs. Barfield, do you have any idea why your son and Maddie led you to believe they were spending time in the mountains when they intended to go to south Florida?"

Her brow arched. "Who told you that?"

"Sara told Kate Bell, Kate told me."

Nora sighed heavily. "Then it's true. I'd heard rumors; kids can't seem to keep secrets." She dabbed at her nose with the tissue again. "I don't know why," she said, "other than they were trying to keep it from Marilyn Harper. She never approved of their relationship."

I'd beat around the bush too long already, so I just spit it out. "I'm aware there's been bad blood between the Harpers and Barfields for a long time. When I spoke with Marilyn Harper she had less than flattering things to say about your family, your son in particular. I was wondering if you could shed some light on that for me."

Nora stood and walked to the window behind the desk. She stared out for a moment, her back to me. When she turned, she crossed her arms under her breasts and lifted a hand to stroke the hollow of her neck. "Marilyn has hated me ever since high school," she said. "I tried hard to be her friend when my family first moved here, but she made it impossible.

"I was voted captain of the cheerleading squad and homecoming queen our senior year. Marilyn couldn't stand me because of that. She was the most selfish, self-centered person you could imagine," she said, voice rising. "She hated the thought of anyone stealing the limelight from her, jealous of anyone else's accomplishments, even her own sister's!

"You wouldn't think it of identical twins, but the only thing those two had in common was their looks. Mynta was sweet and kind; she'd do anything for you. But Marilyn . . . let's just say you wouldn't want to turn your back to her. You might wind up with a knife stuck in it. And she hasn't changed in all these years, not one iota!"

During Nora's tirade it dawned on me where I'd seen her—the *Panthers' Pride*. There was no mistaking the raven-haired beauty standing with hands on hips in front of the cheerleading squad, flashing a pretty smile and sporting a captain's "C" above the left breast of her sweater. She'd been Nora Johnson then, if my memory was correct. Okay, so Nora had stolen some of Marilyn's thunder, but was that cause for such deep hatred?

I recalled my little chat with Marilyn Harper, how she'd ranted about "that woman." So, Nora Johnson had dated George Harper for a while and then lost him to Marilyn Pickron. Or had she, really?

I was about to ask if she remembered Lamar Randall when the phone rang. Nora answered, said a quick "Thank you," and hung up.

"I'm afraid I have to run, Mr. McClellan. My husband and I have business to attend to in Parkersville."

I got up to leave, my chance of talking to Clayton Barfield shot for now. "One quick question before I go?"

"Yes?"

"Marilyn Harper mentioned that you used to date her husband. You think that could have anything to do with why she holds such a grudge against you and your family?"

She frowned and her eyes narrowed to slits. "That's really none of your concern," she said, and then showed me the door.

I had baited Nora Barfield with my last question, and her response was about what I'd expected. I was convinced more than ever that she and George Harper had carried a flame for each other long after they'd married their respective spouses. And I'd give good odds that Brett Barfield was proof.

Marilyn Harper had referred to Brett as "that son of hers," meaning Nora's, not "theirs." Nora herself had said "my boy's boat," not "our boy's" boat. Freudian slips? Maybe. I wouldn't lay my head on the chopping block just yet, but I was as sure as Ivory Soap is pure that Friendly George Harper was Brett Barfield's biological father.

Sheriff Bo Pickron had mentioned that a slick Tallahassee lawyer and somebody high up the food chain of Palmetto County politics had gotten young Barfield off with a slap on the wrist for the marijuana busts. Both arrests had been made in St. George. Who was in a better position to see that things were swept under the rug than the mayor of the city, especially if it involved his own flesh and blood?

I'd been wrong about Chief Ben Merritt; no way was he feeding out of Bo Pickron's trough. But Mayor Harper might be tossing enough slop the chief's way to keep him fat and happy.

CHAPTER 13

I drove straight to the St. George Police Department. Beth had the phone cradled to her ear with a shoulder, tapping on the keyboard while carrying on a conversation that sounded more personal than business. She glanced up but kept to her duties.

"The chief in?"

She held up a finger, said something into the phone about meeting after work, and hung up. She picked the receiver back up and punched a number. "Mr. McClellan is here."

She placed the receiver in the cradle again. "Go right on in."

I tapped on the door and walked in. "Well, Mac, it's been a while," Chief Merritt said without bothering to stand up or offer a hand. "Have a seat. You come across any more bodies or marijuana lately?" He chuckled at his little joke.

"No, just Brett Barfield's boat."

His grin faded. "You found Barfield's boat? Didn't know that. Reckon Sheriff Bocephus is keeping things close to the vest these days."

"Looks that way." I got right to the point. "How did Brett Barfield manage to beat those two arrests for marijuana possession a while back?"

Merritt rolled his chair back a couple of feet and crossed his arms. "Well, now, I don't see what business that is of yours." The corners of his mouth turned down. "Who told you about that?"

"Was he dealing?"

"Whoa, now, we're stepping into some sticky business here," he said, face flushing. "Legal stuff. The boy had a big-shot lawyer, and there was a little matter of lack of evidence." He scooted the chair closer and leaned forward, arms resting on the desktop. "Tell me something, Mac, how come you running around here playing detective all of a sudden?"

"Who said I was?"

"I heard some talk. Not much goes on around here I don't get wind of, one way or another."

"Who was the arresting officer?"

"For what?"

"Brett Barfield. Who was the officer that busted him?"

"Look here, McClellan," he said, his face growing redder, "that's official police business. It don't concern you."

"It's a matter of public record, Chief. I can go to the courthouse if I need to."

His jaw tightened. "Sergeant Tom Mayo. Had to let him go a couple of years back."

I made a mental note of the name. "Why'd you get rid of him?"

"Insubordination and other, shall we say, indiscretions. You ought to know well enough an outfit can't run properly when you got somebody refusing to be a team player."

"How about some details, Chief? From what I know it's not easy to get a civil servant canned."

Merritt slapped the desktop with an open palm. "Damn it, man, you're starting to get on my nerves! You come to my town, happen across a body floating in the bay, and now you're acting like God Almighty himself sticking your nose where it don't belong!"

I took a deep breath and let it out. "You're a servant of the people, Chief Merritt. That means you work for me and the other citizens of St. George. I suppose I could go to the city council, or the mayor's office. There must be minutes of the meeting when this Tom Mayo was terminated."

The chief rocked back in his chair and held his arms out. "Look, Mayo didn't always follow orders, okay? And he got caught planting evidence in a suspect's vehicle. That suit you?"

"Any chance that suspect was Brett Barfield?"

He hesitated a second, chewing on his lower lip. "Could've been, but so what?"

"Where can I find Tom Mayo?"

Merritt planted his hands on the desktop and pushed himself up. "No damn idea. He left town after he was fired. Is that all?"

I got up to leave. He didn't offer a hand, not that I expected him to. "Thanks for the info, Chief."

"Watch your step, McClellan," he said as I turned to go. "I let you slide on that marijuana we found on your boat. Next time I might not feel so generous."

I'd made enemies of the Harpers, the Barfields, and now Ben Merritt. And I wasn't exactly Bo Pickron's closest chum, either. Not a bad week's work for a fledgling undercover officer.

My gut told me Sara Gillman wasn't spilling all she knew when it came to Maddie Harper and Brett Barfield. I was convinced Brett was dealing, or had been, but to who? With the THC found in Maddie's body, chances were better than even she'd been involved, too. Being best friends, I wondered if Maddie had slipped Sara an occasional joint or two now and again. Had Barfield been supplying the younger crowd, high school students? Student parking lots are crammed full these days, and most kids seem to have money to burn. Having graduated from Parkersville High, Brett would've had plenty of contacts and potential customers.

I couldn't risk approaching Sara myself, and I didn't think Kate would be overjoyed at the prospect, but Kate was the best shot I had. Sara looked up to her as a close friend and confidant. If anyone could scrape up any useful info from Sara, it would be Kate. That evening I waited outside Gillman's for Kate to lock up. I got out of the truck and approached her as she dropped the keys in her purse.

"You're out of your dang mind!" she said, after I'd told her my suspicions about Maddie's involvement.

There were a few vehicles still parked in Gillman's lot, probably fishermen out late or down by the docks tending to their boats. I suggested we continue the conversation in my truck.

"There's something I haven't told you," I said when we'd settled in the cab. "The autopsy found evidence of marijuana in Maddie's body."

Kate's eyes grew wide; she frowned and looked away. "I don't believe it, Mac, not Maddie."

"I saw the autopsy report. Pickron showed it to me in his office. There was enough THC in her hair and tissue samples to show she was using not long before she died."

"But . . . the baby."

I tried the high road for Kate's sake. "Maddie probably quit the stuff when she found out she was pregnant, but there was still enough in her system to show she'd been using."

Kate looked down and shook her head. "You think you know someone, and you don't really know them at all."

I reached over and placed my hand on her arm. "It doesn't make Maddie a bad person; she was young, experimenting, kids do stuff."

Kate looked at me and forced a smile. "I guess we weren't exactly little angels all the time ourselves, huh?"

I told Kate about my run-in with Ben Merritt, and how he'd fired Sergeant Tom Mayo for "planting" evidence in Brett's vehicle when he'd busted him for possession. "I need to find this Mayo and hear his side of the story," I said. "I think the guy was set up and took the fall to get Brett off the hook."

Kate sighed and shut her eyes for a second. "But why on earth would Chief Merritt do such a thing?"

I knew Kate wasn't going to like what I had to say. "Because he's on the mayor's payroll, and I'm not just talking about Merritt's salary as police chief. George Harper paid him to keep Brett out of trouble."

Kate pursed her lips and blew out a quick breath. "You're *really* fishing now, Mac. That's ridiculous. The Harpers can't stand the Barfields. Give me one good reason why the mayor would bribe Chief Merritt to help Brett Barfield."

"Because George Harper is Brett Barfield's biological father."

Kate's jaw dropped open, and she glared at me as though I'd slapped her.

"Come on," I said, cranking the engine, "let's go for a little ride."

I turned west onto 98 and drove the few blocks to Canal Park, which is just inside the western edge of the city limits. I turned around, backtracked a half-block east, and parked on the shoulder of the highway.

"Take a look at that billboard," I said, pointing to the Harper Realty sign just ahead with Friendly George's grinning mug.

"It's Mayor Harper. So what?"

"So, this." I reached over, opened the glove box, and handed Kate the photo of Brett from the newspaper.

"You've met Nora Barfield. Take a real good look, Kate. What's that saying? 'It takes two to tango'?"

After Kate recovered from her shock we drove to The Green Parrot and got our favorite table on the beachside deck. We ordered fried grouper sandwich platters and a pitcher of beer, and talked over our upcoming plans while we ate.

It took some convincing, but Kate agreed to gently prod Sara Gillman to find out just what she or her friends knew, if anything, about Brett and Maddie's involvement with marijuana. Kate admitted she'd tried pot herself a few times back in school and decided to gain Sara's trust with that approach.

My gut had been telling me for some time that all those camping trips to the Grand Gator Bay Wilderness Area weren't for pleasure only. I reminded Kate that Sara had gone there with Brett and Maddie at least twice.

"Find out if Sara knows anything about Brett growing pot some-where up there. Tell her it could help us discover who's responsible for what happened to Maddie."

Kate dipped a French fry into ketchup. "Just what are you going to be doing while I'm grilling Sara, Mister Big-Shot Detective?"

"See if I can locate Tom Mayo," I said. "Then I'm going for a hike."

Next morning I spent a fruitless couple of hours asking around town if anyone knew Sergeant Tom Mayo and where he might have moved after leaving St. George. A few business owners remembered him, and most had only good things to say about the man, but nobody knew where he'd relocated. Then I remembered an obvious source I'd overlooked.

I drove to the campground and stopped at the office. Jerry Meadows was sitting on the porch shucking fresh corn from the big garden he and Donna grew out back.

"Sure, I remember Tom," he said, plucking silk from an ear. "Fine young feller; kept a sharp eye on the place for us. Always felt he was done wrong when they fired him."

"Do you remember where he moved to?"

He dropped the shucked ear into a tub and rubbed his stubbled chin. "Let's see, little place just outside of Dothan . . . Headland! That's it, Headland, Alabama, few miles up Highway 431 north of Dothan. Said he had a uncle or some other kin there might could get him on the force."

I thanked Jerry and drove to my trailer with a bag of fresh corn he insisted I take. I grabbed my laptop, got online, and typed *white-pages.com* in the URL block. When the site came up I filled out the required fields and hit "enter." In a few seconds I had a listing for a Thomas Alfred Mayo of Headland, Alabama.

I dialed the area code and phone number. After a couple of rings a woman answered. I made sure I had the correct Tom Mayo's residence, then gave Mrs. Mayo my name and said I was looking into the case her husband had been fired over.

I'll spare the tears and most of the details I listened to, but Tom Mayo was killed in a single-vehicle accident not two months after leaving St. George. The brakes had failed on the family's new car, and to avoid crashing into a stopped school bus Tom opted for a deep ditch, flipped over several times, and died instantly.

So much for getting Sergeant Tom Mayo's side of the story.

CHAPTER 14

That evening I called Kate at home. Gary and Linda Gillman had both been around the marina all day, and she'd only had a few minutes to talk privately with Sara.

"They camped at Little Gator Lake, not Grand Gator," Kate said, then added a few specific directions. "Sara said that Brett went off by himself a couple of times to 'explore.' She remembered that he'd cross through a titi swamp somewhere along the north end of the lake and would be gone for a couple of hours at a time. That's all I had time to learn."

I gave Kate the news about Tom Mayo's untimely demise, then told her I'd be gone for the next couple of days.

"Grand Gator Bay?" she said.

"You been reading my mail?"

"It's not funny, Mac. They don't recommend hiking there alone. It's called Grand Gator for a reason."

"Then come with me."

"I can't," she said. "The tournament starts Friday. We were so dang busy today my head's still swimming. The marina will be swamped this weekend."

I'd forgotten about the City Merchants' Fishing Tournament. According to Kate, it was held annually the weekend before the Fourth of July and was a big money-maker for the community. The Fourth fell on Sunday this year, perfect for a huge crowd to swarm St. George's beaches. Speckled trout was one of several categories, and I'd planned on entering. Tomorrow was Wednesday. I only planned to spend one night at Grand Gator. Unless I ran into some unforeseen trouble, I'd be back by late Thursday.

"I'm leaving in the morning," I said. "If I'm not back by Monday, send a posse."

"Not funny, Mac. You be careful."

"Oh, so you care?"

"Yes, I care. You owe me a steak dinner."

Before daybreak I was up and dressed in a set of my Marine Corps camo utilities, called "fatigues" by the other services. They would be cool enough and should provide some protection from any mosquitoes and sand gnats that wanted to feast on me. I cranked the truck and drove east on Highway 98 for several miles, then turned north onto 319, retracing the route Kate and I had taken on our visit to Wakulla Springs. I passed the Wakulla turnoff and stopped in the little town of Crawfordton to grab a large coffee and a couple of sausage biscuits at a fast-food restaurant. I studied the map Kate had marked as I wolfed down my breakfast. I continued north for another three or four miles, then turned west onto the Forest Service road traced in yellow marker.

The dirt road wound for several miles through stands of tall pines and an occasional island of bald cypress growing in the lower areas. The road gradually narrowed until bushes were clawing both sides of my Silverado. After a mile of paint scraping, the road dead-ended where three sections of old telephone pole were sunk into the ground, blocking what was left of the road. A rusting, bullet-riddled sign on the middle pole read: *No Motorized Vehicles Beyond This Point.*

I checked my watch: a quarter to eight. I turned the truck around and parked to one side of a small clearing that looked like it might hold five or six vehicles, providing most of them were VW Beetles or MINI Coopers. I gathered my pack and other gear from behind the seat, saddled up, and hit the trail, such as it was.

According to Sara, she and Maddie and Brett had disregarded the sign and ridden four-wheelers along this portion of the trail. She couldn't remember just how far they'd traveled before they were forced to abandon them where the trail flooded out. There hadn't been much rain lately, so I was hoping for the best. I didn't relish slogging miles through a watery pathway with moccasins and alligators for company.

Gator Bay wasn't your conventional "bay," like an inlet of a gulf or ocean. This type "bay" was an area of higher ground isolated by swampland, creeks, or rivers, about twenty-five thousand acres in all. There were few accessible ways in or out of the wilderness area, and getting lost was a real possibility. I was glad I had my map and compass. The shotgun slung over my shoulder and the machete hanging from my belt upped my comfort level somewhat, too.

An hour later I was still treading on dry ground. I'd seen what could've passed for a side trail a few minutes back. I remembered Sara not being certain which trail they'd taken after parking the illegal four-wheelers and setting out on foot. I kept going, thinking that if I didn't hit water or find another side trail soon, I'd double back and try that one. I wished now I'd invested in a GPS.

Another half hour, and the trail began to squish under my feet. A couple of hundred yards farther, and I was ankle-deep in water. That's when I spotted a small clearing of higher ground just off to the left. There was evidence of low brush having been tramped down, and I noticed several broken branches. If the water level had been higher when Sara had been here, this would've been a good place to park and hide the four-wheelers.

I fished the compass from a pocket, aligned it on my map, and took a reading. The trail was heading more or less due north at this point. Grand Gator Lake lay more to the northwest, and Little Gator Lake a half mile farther on. Little Gator was where Sara said they'd made camp. From the distance I estimated I'd already walked, there would have to be a trail heading in that direction not too much farther ahead. If not, I'd have to backtrack and try the side trail I'd passed.

I pressed on, keeping my eyes peeled for snakes. I didn't think gators would be a problem along the trail, but cottonmouths were a definite possibility. An occasional squirrel barked in the distance, and birds chattered and flitted in the thick brush on either side of the trail but mostly kept out of sight. So far, mosquitoes and gnats hadn't pestered me enough to break out the bug juice.

Ten minutes later I stopped in my tracks and listened. Voices ahead. I didn't want company. No telling who I might run into out here, so I eased off the trail about twenty yards and squatted behind a clump of saw palmettos that offered good concealment. The chatter grew louder, and in a couple of minutes three hikers came into view. They looked to be college age, walking single-file, a girl with a ponytail sandwiched between two guys. All were humping backpacks. The girl was holding a cell phone to her ear, nodding and laughing at whatever was being said. Each wore shorts, T-shirts, and ball caps. The guy walking tail-end-Charlie and the girl carried walking sticks; the point man had a walking stick in one hand and a machete clutched in the other. I watched them pass out of sight, gave them another two or three minutes, and then eased back onto the trail.

There hadn't been any other vehicles where I'd left my truck. Maybe they'd come in by a different route or had arranged for someone to pick them up. Never too proud to learn a lesson, I unsheathed the machete, cut and trimmed a sapling suitable for a walking stick, and slogged on up the trail. A minute later a large blackish snake slithered across the surface a few feet ahead and disappeared into the brush and trees. It might've been a harmless water snake, but I sure as hell wasn't about to chase after it to find out.

The water was knee-deep when a few minutes later I spotted what looked to be a game trail to my left. I sheathed the machete, grabbed a small tree for support, and scrambled up the two-foot embankment. I leaned my walking stick against a tree, grabbed my map and compass, and shot a reading. The trail led roughly northwest. I checked my watch. I'd been hiking about three hours and figured I'd covered around five or six miles. Odds were good that this was the trail I'd been seeking.

The trail was narrow but less than ankle-deep in most places, with canopy overhanging so low in areas that I was forced to walk bent over. I craned my neck, eyeballing the overhead brush. I damn sure didn't want to wind up wearing a water moccasin as a necktie.

My back was aching when the trail finally gave way to a view of a beautiful lake ringed by magnificent cypress trees growing in the shallows. Grand Gator. The lake was roughly oval, maybe a half mile across from where I stood, and a mile wide end to end. A couple of ospreys circled above, their keen eyes searching the obsidian water for lunch. A dozen or more herons and egrets stalked among cypress knees, ready to spear a meal of their own.

I checked the grass around me for unwanted critters, shed my pack and other gear, and sat down for a rest. I grabbed a water bottle and a two granola bars from my pack and feasted while I studied the nearby surroundings. There were signs of a few old campfires here and there and a frayed clothesline strung between two trees. The sun reflected off a couple of discarded beer cans. So much for the hiker's creed of leaving nothing behind but footprints. According to Sara, she, Maddie, and Brett had walked left—west—to the far end of the lake, and then taken a trail that lay hidden behind twin live oaks on the north side that led to Little Gator Lake.

It wasn't noon yet, so I pulled off my boots and pointed the openings toward the sun to dry. I aired my feet for a while and then fished a dry pair of socks from my pack. In a few minutes I heard the droning of a small airplane. When it came into view there were no visible markings on the wings or fuselage. I watched as it flew over the lake and disappeared to the west. Was someone out for a joyride this beautiful summer day? A student taking lessons maybe, or the law searching the wilderness for marijuana plots?

After spending the better part of an hour resting and watching osprey hover and dive for fish, I put my nearly dry boots back on, saddled up my gear, and headed for the western end of Grand Gator. Reaching the north side, I had no trouble finding the twin live oaks whose sprawling, moss-covered branches spanned a good forty yards combined. A few minutes of searching revealed a narrow trail leading north. The entrance was concealed by a saw palmetto thicket, but the trail was a hell of an upgrade to the one I'd used to reach Grand Gator Lake.

The footpath was only a couple of feet wide and led through a forest of virgin pines towering above an undergrowth of palmetto and other low-growing brush. This was prime diamondback rattlesnake country, so I eyeballed the trail ahead and to both sides for any sign of movement or "branches" that might have fangs at one end and rattles on the other. I was beginning to wish I'd taken the salesman's advice at Redmond's Sporting Goods and bought those snake boots he'd recommended.

Little Gator Lake was a sight to behold. Maybe a third the size of Grand Gator, the water was a clear, pristine blue with a white sandy bottom, a sure indication of being spring-fed. Almost circular, most of the southern half was clear of trees and grass, with a narrow strip of sugar-white sand rivaling what I'd seen of the beach along Five-Mile Island. Tall stands of cypress and grasses dominated the northern end, providing good cover for fish and other amphibious critters. Any gators living in this lake would be drawn naturally to that side for their food source. I could see why Maddie Harper had been so fond of this place; Brett Barfield, too, but I still suspected there was more than the scenery that drew him here so often.

I followed the shore westward until I came to a cleared area not far off the lake. Near the middle was a fire pit circled with several limestone rocks the size of unabridged dictionaries. Where there are springs, there's limestone. Someone had most likely plucked these from the lake bottom. I thought of the autopsy report. Had someone bashed Maddie Harper in the head with one of these very rocks?

The clearing would be a fine location to make camp, but this was no joy trip. No sense inviting trouble, so I decided to pitch my tent where it would be harder to see if other hikers or pot farmers happened to be in the area. I moved away from the lake and searched the edge of the surrounding woods. I soon found a small natural clearing with enough brush around that would make it difficult to spot unless a person just happened to stumble onto it. I unloaded my gear and used the machete to clear away enough brush so that the tent would easily fit with room to spare on all sides.

Twenty minutes later the tent was pitched. I walked down to the lake and looked back toward my bivouac. I'd chosen well; the brushy area looked natural with no sign of the tent. I wouldn't be making a fire, so I didn't bother gathering wood. I'd packed light: jerky, granola, and a couple of candy bars. I had plenty of water and a flask of good scotch. Home sweet home.

A little before three that afternoon I was hoofing it around to the north shore of Little Gator Lake. I left the walking stick back at camp. I had the machete on my belt, and my shotgun slung upside down over my right shoulder. A quick flip up, and it would be in position to fire from the hip. There were still about four hours of daylight left, but I'd brought along a pocket-size flashlight just in case.

Finding the titi thicket was a breeze, but it took nearly fifteen minutes of tramping up and down and sticking my head into the thick brush before I finally spotted the trail. I worked my way into the titi looking for an occasional branch or limb that had been cut and tossed aside, making just enough room to squeeze through the dense tangle. Making matters worse was the thick canopy, turning bright afternoon into twilight. The ground was wet and spongy, over my ankles in places, but the dry spell spared me from wading through any knee-deep swamp. I did my best to not think about snakes.

The bugs that had left me alone most of the day finally rang the dinner bell. I swatted at swarms of mosquitoes buzzing around my head. That only seemed to draw more to the feast, so I pulled out the bug juice and slathered it on every bare inch of skin I had except my eyeballs. Dripping sweat soon took care of that.

I kept following the trail, made harder now by my stinging eyes. It seemed like I'd been humping the titi swamp all day before I finally saw sunlight filtering through the thicket ahead. In a few more minutes I was out of the swamp and standing at the edge of a forest of huge pines.

I pulled a paper towel from the stuffed baggie I'd brought along for nature's call, tore off a strip, and stuck it onto a branch where I'd come out of the titi. I wiped my burning eyes with the rest of the towel and checked my watch. Ten to four. It had taken a half-hour to get through the thicket. I walked along the brush line edging the pine forest looking for any obvious pathways into it. After a few minutes I found what looked to be a game trail and started in. I'd taken maybe ten or twelve steps when my boot froze in midair.

Tripwire!

I'd seen plenty of them during the fight for Fallujah. The mujahedeen were experts at booby-trapping buildings using tripwires attached to IEDs. Too many good Marines had been blown away by them.

I eased my foot down and stepped back, then took a knee to get a closer look. It was thin stainless wire, light gauge. I'd seen the same type before, and recently. Unless I was mistaken, this was leader wire, used mostly for king and Spanish mackerel fishing. I'd watched Lamar make several leaders from a large roll for the Gillmans' store. That didn't implicate Lamar, but Brett Barfield's family was in the fishing business, and I damn well knew he'd been here.

The wire ran across the trail about ankle high and disappeared into the brush on either side. I eased parallel along the wire to see what it was attached to. It might be bad news or maybe just some tin cans with rocks inside to act as a warning that someone was approaching. The wire ended next to a small tree about ten feet off the trail. Being as careful as I could, I pulled the brush away. The hair on the back of my neck rose up when I spotted what was either a flare or a stick of dynamite. I wasn't risking my ass to find out which. I pulled my cell phone out of the plastic bag and snapped a few pictures. Then I tore a strip of paper towel to mark the wire where it crossed the trail and moved on.

I was on high alert now, my adrenaline kicking in like I was on a combat patrol back in Iraq. Somebody was up to no good around here, or had been. I eased along, eyeballs peeled, sweeping the trail closely for wires or other danger. Forty yards ahead I spotted another wire. I moved over carefully, this time testing the ground first for solid footing. Some of the old salts I'd served with who'd been in the Corps during Vietnam had mentioned how the Viet Cong would often dig punji pits just past their tripwired booby traps. If a soldier or Marine spotted the wire and stepped over it, the next step might find his foot plunging into a camouflaged pit filled with sharp, poison-coated stakes.

The ground held. I marked the wire, took a deep breath, and kept going. I considered getting off the trail and working my way through the underbrush but decided I'd rather watch out for wires than rattlers. Every few yards I stopped and scanned the area for signs of marijuana plants. I'd read on the Internet how growers will often hide their crop between rows of pines; enough sunlight filters through for good growth while offering excellent concealment from aerial surveillance. These mammoth pines were old growth. Loggers had likely never laid eyes on them, but it looked like an ideal place to hide a pot plot.

I spent a good hour searching the area. I didn't come across any more tripwires or punji pits, but I didn't find any marijuana plants either. I was just about ready to give up the search and head back when a burlap bag lying behind some bushes just off the trail caught my eye. I gave the area a good visual going over and then worked my way around a bush to the bag. It was the same type used by oystermen, and it wasn't empty.

I nudged it with my boot and then flipped it over with the shotgun barrel. No movement or buzzing, so I figured it didn't contain a nest of diamondbacks. I reached down, grabbed the bag by the bottom corners, and lifted it. Stacks of small black plastic containers spilled onto the forest floor, the kind tomato and pepper and other seedlings come in. I took a quick count; there were around four dozen. A few similar bagfuls, and you could have one hell of a profitable marijuana crop.

I grabbed my phone again and snapped a few more pictures, then headed back to camp.

I made it back to my bivouac before dark. Nobody was around, so I stripped down and took a quick dip in Little Gator Lake to wash off the sweat and bug juice. Inside the tent, I put on a fresh set of utilities, ate a pack of jerky, and washed it down with scotch. Not a bad combo after a long trek through the wilderness. I tried calling Kate to let her know I was still among the living, but I couldn't pick up a signal from my campsite. I was bushed, and sleep came easy.

The first day of July dawned hot and muggy. I broke camp before the sun topped the trees, saddled up, and hit the trail. The hike back was uneventful except for a three-foot water moccasin I spotted about a mile from trail's end that posed no threat. It was still a relief when I got back to my truck and found it safe. I stopped in Crawfordton again for breakfast and was back in St. George just past one.

Inside my trailer, I showered and put on a pair of shorts and T-shirt. I started to shave but then decided what the hell. I liked the look of the two-days' growth and let it go.

The parking lot at Gillman's was damn near full when I pulled in at two-thirty. The store was buzzing with tourists in town for the big weekend. Kate was behind the counter working the register for a long line of customers, too busy to notice me when I'd come in. Sara was manning a table in front of a large banner announcing registration for the fishing tournament. I walked over and stood in line.

"Oh, Mr. Mac," she said, breaking eye contact when she saw it was me at the head of the line. "What categories are you entering?" The usual smile and perkiness in her voice were missing. I guess I was fairly high on her poop list at the moment.

I flashed a smile, hoping to break the icicles loose. "Just speckled trout, single boater."

"That'll be fifty-five dollars, please." I was surprised I couldn't see the frostiness in Sara's breath as she jotted down my entry on the proper sign-up sheet.

I counted out the correct cash and laid it on the table in front of her. "There you go."

"Thank you," she said and handed me a flyer with the contest rules without looking up. "The weigh-in deadline is seven o'clock, Friday and Saturday evening."

I idled down the aisle where the lures were located and picked up a silver MirrOlure and a blue and silver Rapala, then moved to the end of the line Kate was working. I hoped I'd get a warmer welcome from her.

When I was a few customers away Kate glanced over and smiled. At least I'd managed to avoid stepping in her piss pot. When I got to the register I handed her the lures. "Movie and dinner tonight, O'Malley's?"

"Can't, Mac. I don't get off until seven." She did a double-take. "Are you growing a beard?"

"Maybe. You like it?"

"Yeah, I think I do."

"The movie's not until nine. Pick you up at eight-fifteen?"

She took my money and gave me the change, my bagged lures, and a smile. "Okay, see you then."

O'Malley's wasn't your ordinary movie theater. Instead of rows upon rows of seats, there were tables and chairs where couples or small groups could sit together and enjoy a dinner menu or regular movie fare while watching classic films from yesteryear. Tonight's feature was *Casablanca*, which I'm sure Kate had probably seen as many times as I had. But hell, can you ever get too much Bogie?

During the drive to Parkersville I filled Kate in on what I'd found during my little excursion to Grand Gator Bay and showed her the photos I'd taken.

"That's not the Brett Barfield I know," she said after looking at the tripwires strung across the trail. "Okay, maybe he was growing marijuana, and maybe he dragged Maddie into that mess, but I still can't imagine him blowing people up."

"They could've been dummy wires just to scare people away," I said, "but I wasn't about to risk my butt to find out."

We agreed to put off any further discussion about the case for the time being and enjoy our dinner and movie. The roast beef sandwich platters and pitcher of beer hit the spot, and the company couldn't be beat. By the time Rick Blaine and Captain Renault walked off into the fog, to paraphrase Rick's closing line, I was sure Kate and I were beginning a beautiful friendship.

After the movie Kate took my arm in hers as we strolled back to the truck. Things were beginning to look promising. I turned onto Main Street and headed for the highway, hoping tonight might just be the night for Kate and me to move our relationship a step farther. We'd just passed the Commerce Bank when something caught my eye. I took the first right and turned right again at the next block.

"Where on earth are we going?"

"Don't stare, but take a look down the alleyway behind the bank when we pass by," I said. "Tell me what you see."

I slowed a little as we drove past the alley that was lit by a nearby streetlamp. Kate turned her head just enough to see. "It's Chief Merritt. So what?"

"Yeah, in Parkersville, not St. George. Who's the other guy?" I circled on around the block and passed in front of the bank again so Kate could get another look.

"Hey . . . that's Clayton Barfield, Brett's dad."

I thought I recognized him from one of the photos on the wall the day I'd visited Barfield Fisheries. I glanced at Kate. "You got any idea why a grieving father would be laughing it up with the chief of police in an alleyway at eleven-thirty at night?"

CHAPTER 15

"You know what I'm starting to believe?" I said as I pulled into Kate's driveway.

"What?"

I rolled down the power windows and switched off the engine, rested both hands on top of the steering wheel, and stared through the windshield at Kate's house. "That Brett Barfield is still alive."

Kate unbuckled her seat belt and slid closer. She placed a hand atop mine. "Then you think he's responsible for what happened to Maddie?"

I glanced at her, then out the windshield again. "I don't know what to think. But if he's dead, why the hell would his father and Ben Merritt be laughing it up in that alley?"

"I still say they were arguing, not laughing," Kate said, moving her hand. "It looked like it to me, anyway. Besides, you said George Harper is Brett's father."

I nodded. "Biological father. I'd bet on it. But even if Barfield found out his wife *had* fooled around, he still raised Brett like his own son. You don't just throw away twenty-one years. That man in the alley didn't strike me as someone who's just lost a son. My guess is Brett's alive, and Clayton Barfield knows it."

Kate let out a deep breath. "They were arguing, Mac. And I don't mean to bring up a sore subject, but shouldn't you let Bo Pickron in on what you've learned? You're supposed to be working for him."

With everything that had been happening I'd almost forgotten about Bocephus. "Yeah, I'll touch base with him Monday. He'll be busy enough this weekend with this crowd down for the Fourth."

For a moment neither of us spoke. Then Kate leaned over and gave me a quick peck on my stubbled cheek. "You want to come in?"

Why the hell did I have to drive by that bank in Parkersville? Seeing Barfield and the chief together had blown the romance right out of the air. I looked at my watch. "It's midnight, and I'm guessing you've got to be at work early. Rain check?"

"Sure." Kate grabbed her purse and opened the door. "I had a nice time tonight."

"Me too. Thanks."

She shut the door and leaned through the open window. "Are you going out in the morning?"

Heat lightning had been flaring in the clouds over the gulf during our drive back to St. George, and the wind had picked up. "I paid my entry fee. What's this weather supposed to do?"

Kate gave the sky a quick look. The wind lifted her hair, blowing it off her neck and shoulders. "It's iffy," she said. "NOAA said a low-pressure system is trying to form in the central gulf. They're giving three to five offshore, choppy in the bay. Dang lousy timing for the tournament."

"Guess I'll drive down to the park and take a look first thing in the morning. See you tomorrow."

"Night, Mac," Kate said and headed for her house. "Oh, I almost forgot." She turned and walked to my side of the truck. "Guess who the Gillmans hired?"

"Sandra Bullock?" Ask a silly question, get a silly answer.

"Funny, ha ha. Hey, do you have a thing for her?"

"She's easy on the eyes."

Kate gave my arm a playful slap. "No, not Sandra Bullock. Tonya Randall, Lamar's daughter. She starts tomorrow."

I was up before daylight, made a pot of coffee, filled my thermos, and drove to Canal Park. I parked and walked out onto the seawall. The wind was blowing steady out of the west or southwest, and even in the pale light of dawn I could see whitecaps dancing far out in the bay. I was still after my gator trout; the fifteen-hundred-dollar prize for first place in the speck category was tempting, but I decided the fifty-five-buck entry fee wasn't worth risking the rental boat or my own ass over. I'd wait for the conditions to improve. If worse came to worse, I could always drive to the island and wade the grass flats.

I watched as a couple of charter boats eased out of the canal and over the sandbar, then throttled up and headed southwest, bucking over the choppy bay waters. These were the big-money boys, heading for the open gulf and the serious prize money categories like snapper and grouper or trolling species. It was still dark enough that they were burning their running lights.

I waited until they were as small as toy bathtub boats, then tossed the dregs of my coffee and headed back to the truck. I drove past the marina; the lights inside the store weren't on yet. I wanted to talk to Kate, but I knew she'd be busy all day, probably even work through her lunch hour. I had my fishing gear and boots packed, so I decided to head to Five-Mile Island and try my luck from shore.

Learning that Tonya Randall would be working with Kate and Sara at the marina store was a stroke of good luck. Kate promised she'd keep her eyes and ears open around the two teenagers. There was a chance she might pick up some useful bit of info by careful eavesdropping that neither of the girls would be willing to volunteer openly.

Seeing Ben Merritt and Clayton Barfield last night had turned my theory about the case on its head. I'd assumed all along that Brett was dead, and he still might be, but Barfield's behavior last night didn't point that way. Of course Kate kept insisting the two were arguing, but that's not the way I saw it. I was sure of Brett's involvement with marijuana, but I'd thought his was a small-scale independent operation—growing and selling what he could handle alone or maybe with one or two trusted cohorts. The fewer the better in that type of business; less chance of someone's big mouth spilling info.

Was Clayton Barfield running drugs? I recalled my heated meeting with Sheriff Pickron after I'd visited his sister, Marilyn Harper. He'd mentioned how Barfield had worked hard to turn his family's struggling business into one of the most successful on the Gulf Coast. Had Barfield's success come entirely from long hours of hard work and sweat, or was there more to this rags-to-riches story than met the eye? A fleet of fishing vessels would provide the perfect means to smuggle a big score of marijuana or other drugs into the country. Meet a supply boat miles out in the gulf, stash the drugs under the false bottom of fish boxes with tons of fish and ice on top, then motor your "catch" right through St. George Bay to home port at Barfield Fisheries. It made sense, and it had been done before. While I was researching Panama Red on the Internet I came across just such a scenario that had been pulled off successfully on the West Coast.

Why not here, especially if you had the local authorities in your pocket?

I stopped for breakfast at the Trade Winds Restaurant. Figured if I was a paying customer they wouldn't mind me parking and fishing there. I planned to fish until noon or one, then break for lunch at the restaurant, too.

After I'd eaten I pulled on my boots, grabbed my gear, and walked down behind the cabins to the shore. The hair on the back of my neck prickled, and I tried not to stare at the area where I'd hooked Maddie's body. I walked west along the shore for about a hundred yards, rigged up, and waded out to the side of a large grassy patch. I started casting, but my heart wasn't in it. There was a conundrum that kept bugging the hell out of me as I ran what I knew, or thought I knew, about the case through my mind again: The Barfields and Harpers got along about as well as the Hatfields and McCoys, yet Chief Ben Merritt appeared to be feeding from both families' troughs. If my theory was correct about George Harper being Brett's biological father, then Harper had paid Merritt to keep his son out of trouble more than once. Beating a simple possession charge was one thing, but Chief Merritt had obviously framed his own man, Sergeant Tom Mayo, after Mayo busted young

Barfield with a considerable amount of pot in his vehicle. It wound up costing Tom Mayo his job and maybe his life.

Marilyn Harper hated the Barfields with a passion, especially Nora and Brett, who she most likely knew was her husband's illegitimate son. George, the former high school stud who drove the fancy cars and whose daddy owned a successful auto dealership, had once dated Nora Johnson but dumped her for Marilyn Pickron, one of the local sheriff's pretty and popular twin daughters. That had been while the Barfields were struggling and the Harpers were in high clover. But later, George took over the family's auto business and ran it into the ground. The deaths of Marilyn's twin sister and brother-in-law had remedied that problem, bailing George out of debt and handing him and Marilyn a beautiful home and successful real estate business.

The problem was, the majority of the Harper money would become Maddie's when she turned twenty-one, and with Maddie and Brett expecting a child and planning to marry, the Barfield family would be wed into the Harper fortune.

If Chief Merritt was on the take from George Harper to keep Brett out of trouble, wouldn't Clayton Barfield be aware of it and be grateful for whatever political pull George used to help their "mutual" son? Was Friendly George in cahoots with Barfield's drug operation? After all, he stood to lose a ton when Maddie turned twenty-one. Maybe the drug operation was a way for him to build a tidy nest egg once Maddie claimed her inheritance. But knocking off his niece, who he'd raised like a daughter—I just couldn't buy that. Then again, at the funeral George hadn't seemed all that broken up over poor Maddie's death.

And what about Lamar Randall—where did he fit into all this? He had "Mare"—Marilyn Pickron Harper's nickname—stenciled across the fingers of his right hand. Was it just a coincidence that he'd suffered an eye injury around the same time that Maddie died and Brett disappeared? He'd obviously had a thing for Marilyn at one time, and Marilyn hated Brett. Could Marilyn Harper have used Lamar's unrequited love for her to sic him on Brett, to pressure Brett to leave Maddie alone? My puzzle was jumbled worse than ever, and there were more than a few pieces missing.

My head was about to bust wide open trying to make heads and tails out of this scrambled mess when my cell phone rang. I unbuttoned my shirt pocket and grabbed the phone. "This is Mac."

"Hello, Mac? Mac, is that you?"

"Yeah, speaking," I said. The connection wasn't the greatest, and I didn't recognize the voice.

"Mac? This is Jerry Meadows. You best get over here quick as you can. Your trailer's on fire."

By the time I drove back to Gulf Pines Campground there wasn't much left of my home-sweet-home. A blackened frame piled with twisted, melted siding resting on tireless rims was about all there was to see. Luckily, the volunteer fire department had arrived in time to keep the LP cylinders hosed down so they wouldn't explode. The hitch wasn't in bad shape either. It might be worth a couple of bucks in scrap metal. If somebody was trying to send me a message, they'd sure done a bang-up job of it.

I was standing just across the road from the still-smoking ruins talking with Jerry and Donna when Ben Merritt's blue-and-white cruiser drove up. The driver's side door opened, and the shocks sighed with relief as the chief hefted himself out of the vehicle. The passenger door opened, and Patrolman Owens exited.

"Well, Mac," the chief said as he lumbered over, "looks like bad luck follows you around like an albatross."

"Looks that way, Chief," I said. "Least I got insurance."

"You want me to take some pictures, Chief?" Owens said to Merritt, waving a camera in his face.

"Yeah, go take some damn pictures, but don't go touching nothing," his boss said.

"You forget to unplug your coffee pot or something this morning?" Merritt said, a smirk spreading across his face.

"Not that I know of. I'd put my money on an arsonist," I said, staring him down. "Jerry here says Tom Mayo used to keep a good eye on this place." Over the chief's shoulder I saw Owens stop and glance my way at the mention of Tom Mayo's name. "You boys ought to be out patrolling more often to keep things like this from happening."

"And you ought to keep your nose out of where it don't belong," Merritt snapped back. "What'd the fire chief have to say?"

"Beats me," I said. "I haven't seen him."

"Chief Daniel done been here and gone," Jerry said.

"Well, reckon I'll just go have a little talk with him," Merritt said. He cut loose a loud whistle. Patrolman Owens looked over at us.

"You about done, boy?"

"I took a few, Chief."

"Well, let's go then."

They climbed into the cruiser and slammed the doors. Ben Merritt leaned out his window. "Sorry about your camper there, Mac," he said, grinning. "Be seeing you."

After Merritt left and Jerry and Donna went back to their duties running the campground, I walked around the burned hulk of my late home wondering what the hell I was going to do now. I needed to call about the insurance and get a room somewhere, that much was for sure. I felt like buying a couple of six-packs and heading for the beach to stare at bikinis and get buzzed, but there was no sense in putting off the inevitable.

As I turned back to my truck something lying near the electrical box at the edge of the scorched grass caught my eye. I bent down and picked it up: a man's tortoiseshell pocket comb, partially melted, with *KENT* stamped in the center inside an oval. Funny that I'd never noticed it before, since Jerry was a stickler about keeping the grass and weeds trimmed around the sites. Maybe one of the firefighters had lost it. I tossed it onto the burned carcass of my home and headed for the Silverado.

I turned down Jerry and Donna's offer to stay with them until I figured out what I was going to do. I borrowed their phone book and got the number of my insurance company. I called and explained what had happened. The agent I spoke with looked up my policy and told me not to worry, they'd have an adjuster onsite first thing Monday morning, even though it was a business holiday. Meanwhile, my coverage included the cost of motel rental if that's what I chose to do; just be sure to save all the receipts.

I apologized to Jerry and Donna for the inconvenience the fire had caused, assured them I would honor my lease, and then went room hunting. I was shit out of luck. There wasn't a motel or hotel room in all of St. George that wasn't booked through the Fourth. I thought about driving to Parkersville and looking there but decided to go see Kate first.

It was a quarter to two when I found a parking spot and entered the store. Kate was working the register; Sara and a cute young brunette who I assumed was Tonya Randall were ambling about the aisles, straightening clothes and assisting shoppers. Kate saw me and waved me over.

"Dang, Mac, is it true?" she said, after checking out a customer.

"Is what true?"

She let out a breath, frowned, and almost rolled her eyes. "Your trailer—did it burn up?"

"Down's more like it. How'd you hear about it?"

"One of your neighbors was in this morning," she said. I stood aside for a customer buying a couple of T-shirts and a pair of shorts.

"We heard the sirens this morning," Kate said when she'd completed the transaction. "A little later this woman came in and said there'd been a fire at Gulf Pines Campground. She said the camper belonged to a Mr. McClellan. I was worried sick until she said your truck was gone and the camper was empty."

"You had lunch yet?"

Kate shook her head and glanced at the clock behind her. "Give me five minutes. I'll tell Linda I need a break. Meet you at the bench out front."

I walked out to the bench that sat under a large awning in front of the store, keeping a wary eye out for the feathered dive-bombers. It was only a few feet from where they'd launched their attack several weeks back. It had been a while since I'd seen them; hopefully their young had fledged and they had other business to attend to.

In a couple of minutes Kate came out carrying her purse. "I've got a half hour," she said. "I'm starved. Let's go get a quick lunch."

We hustled across the street to the sandwich shop and found an empty booth. Kate ordered a shrimp basket and iced tea; I'd lost my appetite and settled for a beer.

"You can stay with me for a few days," she said when I told her how I'd struck out finding a room. "Chances are Parkersville is booked solid, too."

She saw my grin. "I've got an extra room, Mr. McClellan," she said, fighting back a smile. "Besides, you're a perfect gentleman, remember?"

"I'll think about it, Miss Bell."

The talk grew more serious when I told Kate about Chief Merritt's friendly little visit. She reached across the table and touched my hand. "Mac, why don't you tell Bo you're through looking into Maddie's case? If somebody did set the fire, who knows what they might try next? It's just not worth it. Let the law handle things."

I waited as the waitress placed our order on the table.

I grabbed one of Kate's shrimp and dipped it in a container of tartar sauce. "One, we don't know for sure that the fire was anything more than an accident. Two, if somebody did set the fire and they wanted me dead, they would've done it at night while I was sleeping. And three, it's gotten a little too personal for me to back off now. I'm the one who found Maddie. That day at her funeral something came over me. I can't explain it, but I also can't just up and quit. I feel like I owe it to Maddie to do what I can do."

Kate dipped a shrimp into a small cup of cocktail sauce. "You're as stubborn as a dang mule," she said, her green eyes glaring into mine.

I grinned and tipped my bottle to her. "Hee-haw."

CHAPTER 16

Monday morning at nine sharp I met the insurance agent at the campground. The fire inspector's report stated there was no evidence of an accelerant that might have been used to set the fire. Accidental, most likely caused by an electrical short was what he'd signed off on. For obvious reasons I had my doubts but kept my mouth shut.

The insurance man had no qualms with the inspector's report, which was lucky for me. If arson had been suspected, there was no telling how long the investigation might take, plus I'd have to go through the trouble of proving I didn't torch the camper myself. The agent did his thing and had me sign some paperwork. A check for fifteen thousand plus would be in the mail soon.

I gave the LP cylinders to Jerry, asked him to have the mess hauled off and send me the bill. When my check arrived I planned to buy another camper and park it on site 44.

For the first time in my life I was homeless. I'd joined the Marines right out of high school, and the Corps had been my home for the past twenty-four years. My ex wound up with the beautiful retirement house we'd planned and built on the New River outside of Jacksonville, North Carolina. Jill had wanted and instigated the divorce, but I was willing to give up my interest in the house in exchange for her agreeing not to mess with my retirement pay. I made sure to get it in writing, of course. Not a bad deal, the more I thought about it.

Kate had been good enough to put up with me as her houseguest for the weekend. She said I was welcome to stay as long as I liked, but even though I'd behaved myself I didn't want to overstay my welcome or start tongues wagging. I'd get a room somewhere until the insurance came through.

I had my truck, the clothes on my back, plus a set of camos and boots stashed behind the seat of my pickup. I also possessed three fishing rods and reels, tackle box, the shotgun, and my cell phone. My laptop, digital camera, and other worldly goods were reduced to melted plastic or ashes in the blackened heap of my Grey Wolf camper. I'd been wearing the same shorts and shirt since Friday. I'd washed and dried them once while Kate was at work, but if I didn't get some new clothes soon, she was liable to disown me. It was time to spend some plastic. I headed for the Wal-Mart in Parkersville.

I grabbed two pairs of jeans, some skivvies, several sets of shorts and shirts that I could mix and match, and tossed them into the shopping cart. A comb, couple of toothbrushes, paste, and deodorant joined the crowd. I added a pack of disposable razors, too. Kate still liked the beard, but it was creeping up my cheeks and down my neck. A box of mustache and beard coloring caught my attention. I'd noticed a little salt among my reddish-blond whiskers. I picked it up and read the instructions, then put it back on the shelf. What the hell, maybe Kate thought a little gray made me look distinguished.

I was headed back to my truck when somebody called my name from behind. I turned and saw a tall young man approaching. "Mr. McClellan?" he said again.

Only when he was a few feet away did I recognize who it was. "Patrolman Owens. You look different out of uniform."

He held out his hand. I transferred the Wal-Mart bag to my other hand and we shook. "It's J.D., sir. I'm working night shift tonight."

"Chief Merritt got you tailing me on your off time, J.D.?" I was only half-joking.

Owens looked down and shifted his weight from one foot to the other. "No, sir, I just got here and seen you coming out of the store. I been wanting to talk to you, though."

"What about?"

He shoved both hands in his pants pockets and rocked on his toes. "The other day at your trailer, I heard you mention Tom Mayo."

"Yeah, he used to be on the force until your boss had him fired."

"Yes, sir, I know. Mr. Mayo was my basketball coach when I played in the city rec league. He's the main reason I wanted to be a cop, him and my daddy."

Out from under Ben Merritt's shadow, J.D. Owens seemed like a nice enough kid. I hated being the bearer of bad news, but I figured he'd want to know. "Did you know Tom Mayo's dead?"

Owens looked down again and nodded. "Yes, sir, car wreck."

"Yeah, his wife said the brakes failed. Brand-new car, too. Talk about lousy luck."

J.D.'s eyelids quivered like a nervous tic. "My daddy said there was some bad blood between Coach Mayo and Chief Merritt."

I unlocked the truck door and tossed my bag onto the seat. I left the door open to let some of the heat escape. "How would your father know that?"

"Him and Coach Mayo and Chief Merritt were deputy sheriffs together a while, back when Bo Pickron's daddy was sheriff."

"Why did they leave the sheriff's department?"

"Bo's daddy was fixing to retire, and when Bo come back from the war with that big flying medal he won, he decided to run for sheriff. My daddy was ready to retire anyway, but Chief Merritt had wanted the sheriff's job real bad. But with Bo running, he knew he couldn't win. Along about then the police chief left, and Chief Merritt got the job. He talked Coach Mayo into hiring on with him."

My gut told me the kid might be open to some frank talk. Being top turd on Merritt's shit list, I figured I had nothing to lose. "Did you know Brett Barfield or Maddie Harper?" J.D. looked to be somewhere around their age range.

"Yes, sir. Me and Brett graduated together. Maddie was a couple of grades behind us. She got hurt in a bad car wreck when she was little and missed a whole year of school."

"You ever hear any talk about Brett being involved with marijuana?"

Owens pressed his lips together and looked away. "I don't think the chief wants me talking about stuff like that."

"Look, J.D., I already know Brett got busted a couple of times for possession," I said, "and that Tom Mayo was the arresting officer. Your boss made sure the charges didn't stick. And I've got good reason to believe that when Mayo stood up to him about it, Merritt had him canned."

Owens crossed his arms and rocked back and forth on his heels. He looked away again for a few seconds, then down at his feet again. "I might've heard something about Brett."

"Like he was dealing to kids at school?"

Owens nodded, still staring at his feet. "Maybe."

"Maybe?"

The young officer scuffed a shoe against the pavement. "I heard he did. A lot of the kids knew about it, but nobody ever ratted on him. Brett was one of the popular guys."

I chuckled. "Yeah, I bet he was. Did Maddie Harper mean anything to you?"

He looked up, his face pinched. "Yes, sir, she was my friend. She used to help me out in study hall sometimes. I wasn't too good at math. They don't come no sweeter than Maddie was."

It was time to lay my cards on the table. "I'm going to be upfront with you, J.D. You can either run to Chief Merritt with what I'm going to say, or you can keep it between you and me."

Owens uncrossed his arms and looked me square in the eye. "Okay."

"I believe Ben Merritt is up to his neck in drug smuggling, along with the Barfields and maybe Mayor Harper, too. Tom Mayo might have died because he was on to them. I can't prove any of it yet, but I'm getting close. Now, you can either rat me out or keep your mouth shut and your eyes and ears open around the chief and find out what you can."

I locked eyes with the young man. "There, I just handed you my ass on a platter. What you do with it is your choice."

I left the kid with his mouth open and a lot to think about. With an hour to kill until the one-thirty meeting I'd arranged earlier with Bo Pickron,

I stopped at Hardee's for lunch. I ordered an Angus cheeseburger with fries and tea, and flipped through the *USA Today* while I ate.

The war in Afghanistan was still dragging on. IEDs continued to take a heavy toll on our troops. And years after Fallujah, Iraq was still going to hell, too. I remembered an old salt who had fought in Vietnam, how he lamented that our government hadn't learned a damned thing from the sacrifice of over fifty-eight thousand dead plus the untold thousands of wounded in body and mind. From what I was reading now, the sacrifices my Marines had made seemed destined for the same fate.

At one-thirty sharp I walked into the sheriff's office. He leaned across his desk to shake hands, then I took a seat. "I heard about your camper," Pickron said. "You better watch your ass."

"Electrical short, according to the official report. Insurance check's in the mail."

Pickron grunted and shifted some papers on his desk. "You got anything for me?"

"Maybe, if you're willing to listen with an open mind," I said, pulling my cell phone from my pocket. I brought up the photos I'd taken on my trip to Grand Gator Bay and showed them to him. "I found out this was a favorite haunt of Brett Barfield's. He and Maddie used to do a lot of camping up there."

The sheriff stared at the photos a minute and grunted again. "So, you think he was growing pot in the national forest."

"He sure as hell wasn't growing daisies. I've got a witness who went camping with him and Maddie a couple of times. My witness saw Barfield disappear through a titi thicket more than once to get to this place."

"Who's the witness?"

I shook my head. "Can't tell you now. If word got out, it might blow my cover."

Pickron handed the phone back. "This doesn't prove anything."

"No? It places Brett Barfield in an area where there are trip wires on a trail and dozens of seedling containers," I said. "And I'd bet my ass if you sent a team out there and searched the place good, you'd find evidence of marijuana still around somewhere."

He gave a wave of his hand. "It's outside my jurisdiction."

"Well, then, call whoever the hell's jurisdiction it is."

"It still wouldn't prove Barfield's involvement."

Damn, Bocephus could be a stubborn SOB. "I've got another witness who says Brett was dealing to students back in high school."

Pickron's eyebrows arched. "I suppose you can't ID this person either."

"Not until we know more. It could put his or her ass in a sling."

"That all?"

"No, but what've you got for me?" So far this "give and take" had been all me giving and all him taking.

"A couple of investigators are looking into things. If they turn up anything useful, I'll let you know."

I lifted a hand, rubbed my eyes a few seconds, and blew out a breath. "You know, if it was *my* niece who got fished out of the bay, I'd try to make this a two-way street."

"Is that all?" Pickron said again.

"Does the name Tom Mayo mean anything to you?"

He thought about it a minute. "There was a Mayo with the St. George Police a while back. I believe he was let go."

"That's the man. You know why Merritt had him canned?"

The sheriff leaned forward and rested his arms on the desk. "Look, McClellan, that's St. George business. I got enough on my plate handling county—"

"Mayo was the arresting officer when Brett Barfield got busted for possession."

"And your point is?"

"I did my research. The second time, Barfield had enough pot on him to face doing time if convicted. Ben Merritt made sure that didn't happen. I'd give big odds he framed his own officer. Made it look like Mayo planted the pot in Barfield's vehicle."

The sheriff's face squinched up like he had bad gas. "Why would Merritt do that?"

I stared Pickron in the eye. "Because he was on the take, keeping Brett Barfield out of the slammer."

He kicked back in his chair and crossed his arms. "Where's the proof, McClellan? So far all I've got out of you is a bunch of goddamn speculation."

I stood up and pulled out my wallet, found the photo of Brett I'd clipped from the newspaper, and laid it on the desk.

"What's this?" the sheriff said, glancing at it.

"Your brother-in-law's biological son."

"You should've seen the look on Pickron's face when I told him that," I said, as Kate handed me a beer and sat across from me at her kitchen table. She had invited me for supper and given the okay for me to spend another night. I'd let the day get away from me after my meeting with the sheriff.

I grinned, thinking about how red Pickron's face had turned, how his jaw clenched so tight I swore I heard his teeth grinding. "I thought for a minute he was going to arrest me for libel or at least kick me out of his office."

Kate didn't find it funny. "You need to stop making waves, Mac. You've already got Chief Merritt on your butt. You don't need Bo biting it, too." She got up and stirred the pot of spaghetti sauce simmering on the stove. "I thought you two were supposed to be working together, not seeing who can piss off who the most."

I swallowed a swig of beer. "We are. It's just that Pickron won't listen unless you slap him upside the head. Figuratively speaking, I mean."

Kate sat back down and took a sip of red wine. "So, what happened after you slapped him upside the head?"

"He calmed down and listened to me, believe it or not. I gave him the whole spiel about how I think Harper, Barfield, and Merritt are in cahoots with this drug thing. He didn't like it, but after he chewed on it a while he admitted there might be something to it."

"What about Mayor Harper being Brett's real dad?"

"Big skeleton in the closet. Turns out Pickron's known it for years. He said that's why his sister hates the Barfields so much, especially Nora and Brett. Both families have kept it hush-hush for the kids' sake. It's just like I thought—Marilyn puts up with George for his money and their social standing."

"Maddie's money," Kate said, getting up to stir the sauce again.

"Most of it, yeah. That's one reason Pickron bought my theory. He thinks it's plausible that George might've gotten involved in drugs as a hedge against losing most of his brother's money to Maddie."

Kate leaned against the counter, sipped her wine, and frowned. "Except Maddie's dead, and now the Harpers get to keep her inheritance."

"Yeah." I finished my beer. "You're off tomorrow, right?"

"Finally. Why?"

"We're going to Alabama."

CHAPTER 17

After Kate agreed to make the trip with me, I called Mrs. Mayo to see if she'd be up for a visit to talk about her late husband's relationship with Chief Ben Merritt. I wanted Kate along, not only for her company, but I thought Mrs. Mayo might be more comfortable and receptive if another woman was present. Joyce Mayo sounded pleased that someone had taken an interest in Tom's firing and hinted that she had info I might find helpful.

It was about a two-hour drive to Headland. On the way up Kate sprang a big surprise on me. "Maddie didn't smoke marijuana."

I raised my hands off the steering wheel for a second in disgust. "You going to start that again? Her samples say she did."

"Well, she did try smoking it a couple of times, but she didn't care for it. Sara told me all about it Sunday at work."

"Right. Bumblebees can't fly, either."

Kate's eyebrows arched. "What's that supposed to mean?"

"I don't know; bad analogy. Look, the autopsy samples showed she'd been using the crap for a while, so Sara's either ignorant or lying. Get over it."

Kate gave me a light punch on the arm to get my attention. I glanced at her. She flashed a smile. "She made brownies and cookies, Mr. Know-It-All. That's how she was using."

"Are you kidding?" I'd heard of marijuana brownies before but thought it was more urban myth than reality. So much for my expertise in the fine art of marijuana use.

"No. Sometimes Maddie would bake a batch when Sara was spending the night at the Harpers'."

"Right under the Harpers' noses. No pun intended."

"Yeah, but it was easy enough to get away with," Kate said. "The secret was in the oil. Maddie would take a bottle of regular canola oil, add ground-up marijuana to it, and simmer it for a couple of hours, being careful that it didn't boil. That extracted the druggie stuff from the pot. After it cooled, she'd strain the oil back into the bottle. Then all she had to do was follow a regular recipe for brownies or cookies or cake, substituting the pot oil for the same amount of regular oil the recipe called for. And keep the oil hidden from her aunt and uncle, of course."

Nobody doesn't like Sara Lee! jingled through my mind. "Pajama pot parties. I bet Sara Lee wishes she could get a piece of that action."

Kate laughed. "Good one, Mac."

"So, little Miss Gillman was a brownie head too?"

Kate sighed. "Now and then, but she's sworn off it since what happened to Maddie."

I wouldn't bet the family jewels on that oath, but I didn't shoot off my mouth to Kate. "What about Tonya or other kids at their school?"

"Sara didn't mention any names, but she did say other girls would join in sometimes when Maddie would have a big sleepover."

"Bet there was a waiting list a mile long," I muttered.

"What?"

"Nothing, just talking to myself."

Following the directions Joyce Mayo had given me, I turned off Highway 441 onto a county road, crossed a small bridge, and stopped at the third house on the right. It was a double-wide mobile home but sat on a concrete slab and was underskirted with real brick. A large covered porch fronted the house. From the distance of the neighboring houses on either side, I guessed the lot was at least an acre.

Kate followed as I walked up the steps, crossed the porch, and rang the doorbell. In a few seconds the door was opened by a trim woman around fifty with silver-streaked blonde hair pulled back in a ponytail.

"Mac?" We'd gotten past the surname formalities during last night's phone call.

I nodded. "Morning, Joyce." We shook hands. "This is Kate Bell."

They exchanged greetings, and then Joyce smiled and stepped aside. "Y'all come on in."

After Kate and I declined our hostess's offer for coffee or something else to drink, we took seats in the comfortable living room. Right away I noticed a couple of manila envelopes on the coffee table separating the recliner rocker Joyce chose and the sofa where Kate and I sat. There was an awkward moment of silence that Kate broke by commenting on what a nice home Joyce had.

Joyce forced a little smile. "Tom had such plans when we moved up here. There's near two acres out back. He was going to buy a tractor and raise a big garden in his spare time. We were planning on opening a produce stand up the road a ways on property Tom's uncle owns." She sighed. "That all ended with Tom's accident."

"Do you remember a kid named J.D. Owens?" I said. "Your husband coached him when he played basketball in the city recreation league."

She smiled. "J.D.? Sure, he was one of Tom's favorites. He wasn't the best athlete on the team, but Tom was always talking about how J.D. had heart and hustle. He said he'd take that over natural ability any day."

"He's a patrolman with the St. George police now," I said. "J.D. said he'd heard his father mention that there was some bad blood between your husband and Ben Merritt. You got any idea what that might've been about?"

Joyce lifted a hand and massaged her forehead a few seconds. "Oh, my, where to begin?" She clasped her hands in her lap and slowly rocked back and forth in the chair. "Tom and Ben were in the Security Police together in the Air Force, what the Army would call your Military Police? They retired around the same time and went to work for the Palmetto County Sheriff's Department.

"Ben was planning on running for sheriff when Henry Pickron retired, only his son come home a hero from that war over in Africa and got elected instead. Do y'all know Bo?"

Kate and I indicated we did.

"Anyway, Ben took a disliking to the new sheriff, so him and Tom left the county and hired on with the St. George Police. Just a while later the chief resigned and moved on to somewhere, and the city hired Ben as the new chief."

"Did your husband ever mention Ben having any dealings with the mayor, George Harper?" I said.

Joyce pressed her lips together. "Funny you mentioned that. Tom said Ben was always kissing up to the mayor. He never told me why directly, but I think it had something to do with keeping some kids out of trouble. Tom would come home fuming about how Ben wouldn't let him do his job proper.

"Y'all sure you don't want some coffee? I could use a cup."

Kate and I said coffee would be fine; black for both of us.

Joyce returned in a couple of minutes with cups on a tray. After we were served, I decided to get down to the nitty-gritty. "Joyce, did your husband think Ben Merritt was on the take?"

Joyce leaned over the table and added a spoonful of creamer to her cup. "Tom never said so directly," she said, slowly stirring the coffee, "but I got that feeling. He didn't want me getting involved in his work, you see."

I nodded. "Do you think Tom suspected that Ben Merritt might've been involved with drugs? Marijuana, in particular."

Joyce took a sip of coffee and set the cup down. "Tom never come right out and said so, but yes, I think he did." She pointed to one of the envelopes. "He was doing some investigating on his own without Ben knowing about it. Took a bunch of pictures. Y'all have a look and see what you think."

For the next several minutes Kate and I flipped through a couple of dozen black-and-white Polaroids. I couldn't make heads or tails out of some, but a few caused both Kate and me to sit up and take notice.

"Isn't that Mayor Harper sitting in Chief Merritt's car?" Kate said, holding the photo up for a closer look.

"That's Friendly George, all right."

"Look at this one, Mac," Kate said, her voice rising. "That's the *Miss Nora*, one of the Barfield boats."

It was a profile shot taken in poor light conditions but clear enough to make out the name painted on the starboard bow. In the background across the bay I could make out the faint lights of the four-story St. George Hotel. That meant the photo had been snapped from either a boat or from Five-Mile Island.

"And here's one of the chief and Brett Barfield," Kate said. "Brett drove that car when I first came to work for the Gillmans."

I took the photo from Kate and stared at it. Merritt was leaning inside the driver's side window, but there was no mistaking who it was. The driver was mostly blocked and in shadow, but Kate was sure it was young Barfield.

Other photos showed promise, but they would take closer scrutiny to see if they would be of use. A good magnifying glass would help, but if we could get access to a computer photo program we might hit real pay dirt.

I gathered up the photos and stacked them like a deck of cards. "Could we borrow these?" I asked Joyce as I slipped them back into the envelope. "I promise we'll take real good care of them."

"Sure," she said, lowering the cup to her lap. "Y'all keep 'em long as you like. I know my Tom done nothing wrong for them to fire him. Maybe the pictures'll help prove it."

I handed the envelope to Kate, who placed it inside her purse. "What's in the other envelope?" I said.

Joyce frowned. "That's the accident report," she said, her voice breaking a little. "A loose brake line caused the brakes to fail." She paused and dabbed at her eyes. "A school bus was stopped on the road and kids was crossing. My Tom had the choice of running into the bus, hitting the kids or taking to that ditch. It's just like him to do what he done."

Kate told Joyce how sorry she was and what a wonderful man he must have been to sacrifice his life to save others. A couple of minutes later we stood up to leave.

"Oh, there's one thing I almost forgot to mention," Joyce said as we walked onto the porch. "I don't know if it's important or anything, but the day Tom had his accident he'd been in Parkersville to see the sheriff about something or other. I never did find out what it was about, though."

We stopped for lunch at a Subway on the outskirts of Headland, looking through the photos again as we ate. "Wish to hell Tom Mayo had had a decent camera when he took these," I said, squinting at a blurry shot of Ben Merritt and someone I didn't recognize. "You got any kind of photo program on your computer?"

Kate finished a bite of her sandwich and wiped her mouth with a napkin. "Just Picasa. It's a free download. It works okay for general stuff, but I doubt it would do much of what we need. My brother could probably help."

"Your brother?"

"Yeah, Mark, my younger brother. He works in graphics at a print shop in Destin. He's got a Photoshop program at home and access to a lot of other equipment at work. He restores old and damaged photos on the side."

I glanced at the photo again. "These aren't damaged, just lousy quality."

Kate's lips pursed around the straw as she sipped her iced tea. "Stop being so negative." She wiped her hands on a fresh napkin and rummaged in her purse for her cell phone.

"What's this going to cost me?"

She grinned as she dialed a number. "Supper, maybe. Mark owes me."

After leaving the Subway we drove to Kate's hometown and met her brother when he got off work at five. Kate and I followed Mark to a nearby restaurant that featured an in-house brewery and enjoyed a nice meal and specialty beers on the back deck overlooking Destin Harbor.

Thirty-year-old Mark Bell was an amiable guy who shared Kate's auburn hair and fair complexion. We briefly discussed Maddie's case with him, and then he studied the stack of photos and concluded he could enhance many of them.

"There's a few here that might give me trouble, but overall I think you'll be pleased with the results."

He refused when I offered to pay for his services, saying that if it would help Kate, that was good enough for him. "I'll need a few days, maybe a week. I'll give you a call when I'm done, Moolah."

"Moolah?" I said to Kate after we said our good-byes to Mark and headed east on Highway 98 back to St. George.

Kate laughed. "Yeah. That's the nickname my brothers gave me when we were kids. 'The Fabulous Moolah,' greatest woman wrestler of all time."

"Moolah," I said again and busted out laughing.

It was past ten that evening by the time I stopped my Silverado in Kate's driveway. I switched off the engine and got out to walk Kate to the door. "You might as well stay the night," she said.

"I can get a room."

"Why on earth waste all that money on a motel when there's a perfectly good bed right inside?"

"Your neighbors might talk."

Kate unlocked the door and stepped inside. "The Fabulous Moolah says to quit being so dang stubborn and get your butt in here."

Who the hell would dare argue with The Fabulous Moolah?

I was up early and had a loaded omelet and toast ready for breakfast by the time a sleepy-eyed Kate sauntered into the kitchen wearing a bathrobe. We'd stayed up late talking over what we'd learned from Joyce Mayo and wondering where to go or what to do next.

Kate yawned, remembering too late to cover her mouth. "Mmm, smells delicious. A gentleman and a chef to boot."

I divided the omelet onto plates. "Coffee just finished dripping. Grab us a couple of cups."

Kate stifled another yawn as she opened a cabinet for the cups. "Did you get the newspaper?"

"No, I'll go get it."

"If you don't see it, check the shrubbery."

I found the damp rolled-up newspaper lying on the grass next to the steps. Kate had poured the coffee and was sitting at the table sipping hers by the time I got back to the kitchen. I slid the rubber band off and dropped the paper on the table, then grabbed our plates from the counter.

"What on earth!"

I turned around, holding a plate in each hand. Kate was staring at the front page, the color drained from her face. "What is it?"

"Dang, Mac—George Harper is dead!"

CHAPTER 18

*M*ayor Harper found dead at home of apparent suicide.

I set our breakfast aside and pulled my chair next to Kate's so we could read the article together. The half-page account boiled down to this: Marilyn Harper had awakened last evening around eight-thirty in the upstairs bedroom where she'd been resting because of a migraine headache. A few minutes later she'd discovered her husband in his downstairs study, slumped face-down on his desk. Thinking he was asleep, she called to him from the doorway, and when there was no response she walked into the study to find a pool of blood on the desktop and a revolver lying on the carpet beside the chair where he sat.

Mrs. Harper immediately dialed 911, and within minutes a rescue squad was on the scene. Attempts to revive the mayor proved futile; he was rushed to Parkersville Memorial Hospital but was pronounced dead on arrival by the attending emergency room physician.

According to St. George Chief of Police Ben Merritt, the investigating officer at the scene, Mrs. Harper hadn't heard a gunshot or any other disturbance. Earlier that afternoon she'd taken medication for her migraine, and as was her habit, wore a sleeping mask and earplugs to bed.

The spent bullet was found embedded in a nearby bookcase and recovered. The pistol, registered to George Herman Harper, age fifty-one, of St. George, Florida, was collected as evidence and would be examined for fingerprints and ballistics by the FDLE in Tallahassee. An autopsy was pending.

The omelets had gotten cold by the time we finished reading the article. I placed them in the microwave for a minute. Kate picked at hers, too upset to eat much. I ate mine and finished hers while she dressed for work. I scanned the article again. There was no mention of Patrolman J.D. Owens being on the scene. I hoped he was still working the night shift and had been there with Merritt.

After Kate left for work I poured another cup of coffee and sat out on the back deck to try to sort things out. If it *was* a suicide, there would be powder traces on George Harper's gun hand and powder burns where the bullet entered his head. The autopsy would show that, and I was sure Bo Pickron would be on top of it. Whether he would share that info with me was another matter.

But why would Friendly George have offed himself, and now of all times? With Maddie out of the picture, he had control of all his late brother's wealth and property holdings. If he really was involved with the drug operation, his cut was all gravy now that Maddie was dead. He no longer needed a nest egg.

But what if George Harper hadn't been part of the drug mess? Why the hell would he have put a gun to his head and blown his brains out? Guilt maybe, believing his son Brett was dead and that if he would've owned up to being a father to him, things might have turned out differently? Remorse over Maddie?

Okay, what if Harper *had* been part of the drug op but wanted out now that he no longer needed the money? There was always the chance the operation could be busted at any time, and that could mean a lengthy stay in the state or federal pen depending how deep the operation went. At fifty-one, Friendly George wouldn't be around very long to enjoy his newly inherited wealth if he spent the next twenty years in the slammer. What if he'd wanted out, but his compadres said no?

What if it wasn't a suicide at all?

I drove to the post office and checked my box. Credit card offers and the new *Leatherneck* magazine. No insurance check, but it had only been two days since the adjuster had examined the burned hulk of my camper. With everything that had happened, it seemed more like two weeks.

Around noon I called Bo Pickron on his personal cell number. This time he answered, and as he had business to attend to in St. George, we agreed to meet by the seawall at Canal Park at three. The business, he told me, was visiting his bereaved sister and helping her with funeral arrangements. I was waiting when he drove up in his SUV.

I offered my hand and told Pickron I was sorry about Friendly George. He shook my hand, grunted, and walked out onto the seawall. I followed. It was around ninety degrees and humid, but a brisk westerly breeze helped. A small flock of gulls waddled out of our way, and a couple of terns that had been mingling with them lifted their wings and rose up and out over the canal.

"Why didn't you tell me about Tom Mayo coming to see you the same day he had his so-called accident?" I said.

Pickron stopped, folded his arms across his chest, and stared out at the horizon. "You didn't ask."

"I talked with his wife yesterday. She said Mayo suspected that Ben Merritt was up to something, and that Merritt was always kissing up to George Harper."

To my surprise the sheriff didn't say anything, just gazed over the water and nodded.

"She said Merritt wouldn't let her husband do his job properly, so Mayo started snooping around on his own to see what he could find out."

Pickron unfolded his arms and pointed toward the western tip of Five-Mile Island. "George saved my life out there once. I was eleven or twelve at the time. Him and Marilyn were having a picnic on the island and let me tag along. They were lying on the beach working on their tans while I was swimming. I got caught in a rip and tried to fight it and wound up going under. George swam out and somehow found me and pulled me to shore."

It was a touching story, but I wondered what it had to do with anything. "Tom Mayo took several photos. I'm having a specialist do some enhancing."

Pickron nodded, still staring out to sea. "Make sure you keep the originals." He turned and started back to his vehicle.

"Do you think it was a suicide?" I called after him.

He stopped in his tracks and turned around. "We'll find out." Then he climbed into the SUV and took off.

I rented a room for a weekly rate at the beachside Sandcastle Motel and then drove to Kate's. I gathered my clothes and other gear and stowed them in my truck. Back inside, I set the spare key Kate had given me on the kitchen table and locked the door behind me. I called Gillman's Marina to let Kate know where she could find me, then drove to the grocery store, bought a couple of six-packs, and headed back to my room.

I put one of the six-packs in the small refrigerator, then kicked off my shoes and walked down to the beach with the other. I sat on the sand just out of the surf's reach and popped open a beer. I took a sip and gazed at Five-Mile Island in the distance, trying to make sense of my brief conversation with Bo Pickron.

He hadn't questioned anything I'd said. It was almost like he'd come to the conclusion that I was right, without saying so. He hadn't denied meeting with Tom Mayo, hadn't shown surprise that Mayo had been sticking his nose in Ben Merritt's business or that he'd taken photos to back up his suspicions.

Had Pickron listened to Tom Mayo's spiel and then decided not to follow up on anything Mayo told or showed him after learning Mayo was killed on his way home? Or, had he given Mayo the same brush-off he'd given me: "This doesn't prove anything"?

So, Harper once saved Pickron's life. Bully for him. But what was Friendly George supposed to do in front of Bo's sister, let him drown? Okay, maybe that was a little harsh, but Pickron knew Harper was a philandering SOB, and it was his sister that Harper was running around on. Was family-by-marriage just cause to knowingly look the other way when your brother-in-law was screwing around on your blood sister, and padding the pocket of the man covering up for his illegitimate son?

Three beers later I still had no clue.

That evening I was propped up on the bed watching the local ten o'clock news when headlights flashed through the drawn curtains. A car door closed, and a few seconds later someone rapped lightly on my door. Great. I'd left the shotgun behind the seat of my truck. I got up and eased across the room, peeled back the edge of the curtain, and glanced out. It was Kate.

I slid the chain latch free and opened the door, just then remembering I was wearing only my skivvies. "Hold on a second, I'm not dres—"

Kate pushed through the door, wrapped her arms around my neck, and kissed me hard on the lips. "I miss you already, Mac," she whispered and kissed me again as she kicked the door shut behind her. She put both hands on my bare chest and backed me toward the bed until my legs buckled, then curled up in my lap and crushed her lips against mine.

It had been a long time, and all the gentleman drained out of me in those few seconds. I wrapped my arms around Kate, returning kiss for kiss, then slid a hand underneath her shirt and cupped a braless breast. She shuddered when I gave the nipple a gentle squeeze.

Kate pushed away and stood silhouetted in the glare of the television. She stepped out of her flip-flops, lifted her shirt over her head, and slipped off her shorts and panties in one swift motion. She pressed her hands against my chest again and pushed me flat on the mattress.

My skivvies were off in a flash. Kate lay prone against me, panting. To hell with foreplay; maybe next time. I ran my hands down her back and cupped her firm butt. Just as I was ready to position her above me, she giggled.

"What's so damn funny?" I was at full attention and loaded for bear. I'd never claimed to be the world's greatest stud, but I'd never had any real complaints to speak of, either.

"I'm sorry, Mac," Kate said, putting a hand to her mouth to stifle another laugh. She grinned. "It just dawned on me that here we are, naked in bed together, about to make love, and I don't even know your real first name."

"Mac."

Her eyebrows arched. "Mac?"

"Okay, MacArthur. MacArthur Andrew McClellan. And don't even think about laughing."

Kate bit her lower lip. "I won't, I promise." She brushed her lips against my cheek. "Nice to meet you, MacArthur."

"Mac."

"Okay, Mac."

"So, what's yours?"

Kate pushed up on her elbows and smiled, her breasts still pressed against my chest. "Kate."

I slapped her playfully on the rump. "Come on, I told you mine, you tell me yours. Fair is fair, as long as we're playing doctor."

"It's Kate, I swear. No Katherine, no Katrina, no middle name. Just Kate Bell."

"Nice to meet *you*, Just Kate Bell."

Nearly every business in town closed Monday afternoon at two o'clock for Mayor George Herman Harper's funeral. I hadn't heard anything regarding the autopsy from Bo Pickron yet, but I figured he had to know the results since the medical examiner's office had released the body to the family on Saturday. I drove to Parkersville that morning and bought a pair of appropriate slacks, a dress shirt and a matching sports coat. At one-thirty I stopped by Kate's, and we rode together to the funeral.

We had to park almost two blocks away, and it was standing room only inside St. George United Methodist Church. St. George. How fitting. In a back pew a kindly older gentleman surrendered his seat to Kate. I stood behind her, leaning against the rear wall of the sanctuary.

Kate was attending out of respect for Maddie. I was there to people-watch and see who might strike up a conversation with who after the service. Outside, the humidity was oppressive, and the temp was pushing the mid-nineties. With the big double doors of the church standing wide open so those who couldn't find room inside to sit or stand could hear, it was sweltering. I unbuttoned my coat and undid the top two buttons of my shirt, glad I'd opted out of wearing a necktie.

After all the preaching, praying, singing, and several eulogies from the upper crust of St. George's political and social world, I grabbed Kate by the arm and led her to a shady spot under a sprawling live oak a few yards from the front steps.

"Dang, Mac, what's the big hurry?" she said, rubbing her arm just behind the wrist.

I wormed out of my coat and loosened the cuffs of my shirt. "I was about to get heatstroke in there," I said, rolling the sleeves midway up my arms. "Besides, this is a good spot to see who all's here. If you notice anybody talking to somebody interesting, let me know."

We could've saved ourselves the trouble. The receiving line looked to be a mile long, snaking around the side of the church as person after person waited to pay their personal respects to the grieving Widow Harper. From where I stood, she seemed to be holding up much better than she had at her niece's funeral.

Bo Pickron was there, just as he'd been at Maddie's funeral, standing straight and tall in support of his sister. The only interesting thing Kate or I noticed was when Ben Merritt approached the bereaved Mrs. Harper. The sheriff of Palmetto County conveniently found someone to hold a conversation with as the St. George chief of police took Marilyn Harper's hand and whispered something in her ear.

After that little show, Kate and I left.

Wednesday morning I was at Carl's Sandwich Shop across the highway from Gillman's having a BLT for breakfast when my phone rang. It was Bo Pickron.

"The autopsy and the forensics report showed it was a suicide, cut and dried," he said. "The powder marks, blood spray pattern, bullet angle, it all shows George put the pistol to his right temple and pulled the trigger."

"And he was right-handed?"

"Yeah."

So much for my theory that Friendly George's buddies did him in because he wanted out of the drug business. Hell, I wasn't even sure he was involved in that mess at all, other than stuffing Ben Merritt's pocket to keep Brett Barfield out of trouble.

"You got any theories why he would've done it?" I said. "Was he depressed or taking any medications?"

There was a pause. "Keep this quiet. George wasn't on anything that I know of, but my sister was. Her doctor put her on Xanax when Maddie died. But the autopsy showed that George had enough of that shit and booze in his system to knock out a mule. He was the type who kept his emotions inside, but Maddie's death hit him hard. He must've gotten the pills from Marilyn and mixed it with his bourbon. Xanax can cause suicidal thoughts in some people. That could be the reason he wound up killing himself."

"How's your sister holding up?" Pickron was being uncharacteristically cooperative, and I figured it would be polite to ask.

"She's okay; a lot better than with Maddie."

"Have your investigators come up with anything?"

"Nothing you don't already know. What about those photos?"

"No word yet. I'll bring 'em by when they're ready. You might recognize something of interest I don't."

"Later, McClellan." Always the charmer.

That afternoon Mark Bell called Kate at work. The photos were ready. I hoped like hell they'd lead to something. I'd been down enough dead ends already.

CHAPTER 19

After Mark's call Wednesday afternoon Kate asked the Gillmans for the next two days off. She hadn't seen her folks in a while and planned to visit family and bring the photos when she returned Friday night. She invited me along, but my insurance check had arrived in Tuesday's mail. I decided to go trailer shopping instead.

I left early Thursday morning for Tallahassee where a dealer sold the same line of camping trailers I'd had before. By five that evening I was setting up house in my new twenty-two-foot Grey Wolf parked among the pines at site 44. Home-sweet-home again.

I was up at daybreak Friday. I hadn't been fishing since the day my old trailer burned. With Kate away I decided to spend the day wetting a hook. There were only a couple of vehicles in the lot when I arrived at Gillman's. I grabbed my tackle and headed for the docks.

I did a double-take when I saw Lamar gassing up a boat near my slip.

"Hey, no eyepatch," I said. A nasty, wide red scar ran from just above his right eyelid to just under the eye, then made a ninety-degree turn and ended at the outside corner. From the looks of it he was damn lucky he still had the eye. "You know, you don't look as much like Johnny Depp as I thought."

He glanced my way and grinned. "Morning, Mac. Who?"

"Johnny Depp, the guy who played Captain Jack Sparrow, the pirate."

"Oh, him. Tonya's got his poster plastered on her bedroom wall. Thanks for the compliment, I think."

"How's the vision?"

Lamar screwed the gas cap on and stepped off the boat onto the dock. "Still a little blurry, but not bad for a scratched retina."

151

I started the motor. Lamar came over and freed my bow line while I took care of the stern. "Hope you learned your lesson about using safety goggles."

"Damn straight," he said, as I backed out of the slip.

I eased out of the canal, crossed the sandbar, and headed east. I kept about a football field's length off the beach, content to ride the calm bay at low throttle, enjoying the early-morning cool before the heat and humidity set in like a wet wool blanket. I didn't have any wire leaders with me, but I decided to give trolling a try anyway. I tied on the biggest deep-running lure I had in my tackle box, opened the bail on my spinning reel, and let the line trail out behind me. I had no idea how to troll, so I ran off about fifty or sixty yards of mono and closed the bail. I propped the rod against the corner of the stern, made myself as comfortable as I could in the seat, and waited.

In a few minutes a boat approached from the east. When it drew closer I saw it was one of Barfield's boats, about a fifty-footer rigged for longlining. That meant it was headed way out for the deep-water gulf, probably after swordfish or yellow-fin grouper. I wondered if that would be the only haul the boat would be carrying when it returned in a week or so.

I was thinking about Kate and how much I missed her when I heard a rattling behind me. I turned around just in time to see my spinning rod with the hundred-dollar Okuma reel bend, lift off the deck, and slide over the stern into the water. Shit! So much for my trolling skills. I had two other rods aboard, but that combo had cost me damn near two hundred bucks. Well, no use crying over spilt milk—or submarining rod-and-reel outfits.

A few minutes later two more Barfield boats passed by heading for the open gulf. One was also rigged for longlining. The other had several "one-arm bandits" mounted on the rails; its crew was going bottom fishing for snapper or grouper or whatever was in season this time of the year.

I started to rig up again and then decided to hell with fishing. I'd spend the morning taking a little sightseeing excursion around Barfield Fisheries instead. I opened the first beer of the morning and toasted my lost rod and reel. After wishing it a final "bon voyage," I gunned the throttle.

Approaching Barfield Fisheries from the water was impressive. There were five docks about fifty yards long running parallel to each other and about twenty yards apart. The second and fourth docks were shaped like a plus sign with a big crane sitting in the middle of the cross-member. It was easy to see that the cranes could easily boom over to service the two docks on either side. Sunlight glared off the roofs of the aqua buildings that rose in the background.

Pilings ran along the outside of the two outer docks, with room enough for a large boat to fit easily between the pilings and the dock. But what really grabbed my attention was the vinyl-covered chain-link fencing that ran the length of the pilings and disappeared under the water. Between each dock was a gate rigged with metal framing to raise up and fold overhead like a garage door. When I got to within fifty yards or so of the docks I noticed several anchored buoys with signs that read in big bold letters: *NO TRESPASSING BEYOND THIS POINT!*

It didn't take an Einstein clone to figure out the Barfields wanted their privacy. I eased the throttle to idle and quickly rigged up one of my spare rods. I began making a show of fishing, staying in one spot for a few minutes and then puttering along to another. Being as inconspicuous as I could, I snapped several pictures with my cell phone. From this distance the quality would most likely suck, but Kate might be able to do something with them on her computer.

I kept at it for a good half hour, making sure I stayed well outside the warning buoys. I even caught and released several silver trout. A couple of times I noticed men in hardhats staring my way. I waved, hoping they'd take me for a friendly tourist out for a day of fishing. It seemed to have worked because each time they returned my greeting.

Then I noticed a guy at the end of the nearest dock scanning me with a pair of binoculars. I slowly turned my back to him and nonchalantly reeled in my line. I made a show of securing my rod in the rack, putting the motor in gear, and puttering away.

I'd just turned off the TV after watching the late news when my phone rang.

"Mac, I just got home," Kate said. "Can you come over right away? You have to see these photos."

"Aren't you working tomorrow?"

"Yeah, but you'll really want to see what I've got here."

I couldn't resist. "Okay, and if we've got time maybe we can take a look at the photos, too."

"Very funny. What happened to Mac the gentleman?"

"Kate the seductress."

"Just get your butt over here."

I was dressed and at Kate's in fifteen minutes. She gave me a quick kiss at the door and led me into the kitchen. On the table was a stack of 8×12 photos. She picked up the top photo and handed it to me.

"Look at this one and tell me who you see."

I held the photo up and turned it away from the glare of the overhead lights. "I'll be damned!"

What had been one of the fuzzy Polaroids was now a focused shot of Marilyn Harper and Lamar Randall cuddled side-by-side in a late-model Lincoln Continental. There were trees in the background but no landmarks of any kind that I recognized. Marilyn was behind the wheel, with Lamar so close to her you'd be hard-pressed to slip a sheet of card stock between them.

"Now this one," Kate said.

Same vehicle, same location, but their arms were around each other and they were clearly lip-locked.

"There's more," Kate said, thumbing through the stack until she found what she was looking for. "Here."

I took the photo and the magnifying glass Kate handed me. A man with long dark hair and a goatee was walking from the Harper's detached garage toward Tara. Mrs. George Harper was standing in the open doorway, waiting.

"That's Lamar, too, don't you think?" Kate asked.

I studied the man with the magnifying glass. "Unless he has a twin brother."

Two more photos at the Harper residence showed much the same thing, and though the quality wasn't as good, there was no mistaking Lamar. So much for unrequited love. Mare and Lamar were obviously an item, or had been when Tom Mayo snapped these photos.

Kate opened the refrigerator, grabbed two beers, and handed one to me. "I wonder how long that's been going on."

"I don't know. I couldn't find any connection between them in the yearbooks I looked through, but Lamar's had that tattoo a long time. And we know from Bo Pickron that Friendly George was screwing around on Marilyn from the get-go. Maybe she was giving the good mayor a dose of his own medicine."

Kate took a sip of beer and slowly shook her head. "Lamar. I can hardly believe it. I thought he and Debra were happily married."

"I'd be willing to bet Lamar's been Marilyn's lap dog for a long time. If she asked him to jump, he'd bark, 'How high?'"

"Maybe. But still, poor Debra."

I shrugged. "Love is a many-splintered thing."

We spent the next half hour or so poring over the photos. Mark had been right; some of the photos were still so poor we couldn't make heads or tails of them. But there was one shot Kate and I both found real interesting. Two men were standing beside the bed of a pickup truck, and from the gesturing that had been frozen in time, they appeared to be arguing. The photo had been taken at a distance, but the man with his back to the camera looked like our newly-discovered Romeo, Lamar Randall. The other person was in shadow, and his face was partially blocked, but Kate swore it was Brett Barfield.

"See the watch on his wrist?" she said, yawning. "See how the watch face is at the bottom of the wrist? That's how Brett always wore his watch." Kate yawned again. "I'm sorry, Mac, but I can barely keep my eyes open, and I've got to open the store at six-thirty."

I waited for an invitation to stay the night, but all Kate offered was another stifled yawn.

Mark had made two copies of each photo. We agreed it would be wise if Kate kept one set and Joyce Mayo's originals, and I took the other set. I still wasn't convinced my trailer fire was an accident.

"Oh, by the way," I said, heading for my truck, "tell your brother I said he's a genius."

After dinner and drinks at The Green Parrot Saturday evening Kate and I drove back to her house. I'd studied the enhanced photos more that day and had come up with a plan. I still hadn't replaced the laptop I'd lost in the fire, but Kate said we could use hers.

First, Kate uploaded the photos of Barfield Fisheries I'd taken with my phone to her computer; she'd see what improvements she could make with the Picasa program later when she had time. Next, she downloaded Google Earth to her hard drive, and then I entered the address for the Harper residence. I zoomed in until we had a nice close up showing a matchbox-size Tara and the surrounding property. A narrow dirt road ran through the woods beside the Harpers' property line. It would make a nice area to park and do some trespass snooping like Tom Mayo had obviously done.

Kate printed out two copies, and then we did the same with the Barfield photos. I was determined to gain access somehow, even if it meant taking to the water like a fish.

"When is Lamar's day off?" I said as I studied the satellite shot of the Harper place.

"Usually Tuesday or Wednesday. It varies."

"Can you check the schedule and find out for this week?"

"Sure, but don't forget that Debra works the night shift at the hospital. If Lamar is still seeing Marilyn Harper he could be going to her place at night, especially now that she's alone."

"Good point, and thanks a lot. You just increased my workload."

Around noon on Sunday I drove to Parkersville. It was time to spend some more plastic. I spent the better part of an hour at Wal-Mart looking at computers and digital cameras, and settled on an HP laptop and a Lumix camera with a twelve-power zoom lens. I'd gotten a good deal on the camper by buying last year's model still in stock. The leftover cash from the insurance settlement was enough to pay for the laptop and camera.

I pulled out of Wal-Mart and headed for 98. Glancing in the rear-view mirror, I noticed a metallic-black Cadillac pull out behind me about a half block back. I was sure I'd seen that car before, or else its clone, a few days ago when I'd met Bo Pickron at Canal Park for our little chat. It had been parked in front of one of the shelters; some ritzy tourists having a picnic or wetting a hook, I'd assumed. There couldn't be that many Cadillac CTSs in this area. I checked the mirror again.

There were two men sitting in the front, but the sun was glaring off the windshield and I couldn't make out any features. My gut was speaking to me again, so I hung a right a couple of blocks from the highway. Sure enough, the Caddy followed. I took another right. The car was hanging well back, but it made the turn. I drove downtown, noticed Redmond's Sporting Goods was open, and made a left and turned into their small parking lot. I got out and headed for the door. Using my peripheral vision I saw that the black Caddy had pulled over and stopped in a parking space about a block and a half back.

Inside Redmond's, I recognized that the clerk who had tried selling me the snake boots was working behind the counter. "Mr. McClellan, I see you survived your hike into Grand Gator Bay," he said, smiling as I approached. "What can I do for you today?"

"Just window shopping," I said, impressed with his recall. I suppose it went with the territory. "Is there a back entrance?"

His eyes widened a bit, but he motioned to a hallway and door at the back of the store with an exit sign above it. "It locks automatically behind you."

Outside, I cut across an alley and circled back down a side street for a couple of blocks until I was behind the Cadillac. It sat parked a half block ahead. I walked down the sidewalk until I was almost alongside the car. A quick glance told me it was a rental. I rapped my knuckles on the rear fender. Through the tinted glass I saw the guys jerk in surprise. A second later the passenger-side window powered down and a head with thinning, sandy-blond hair stuck out a bit to get a better look at me.

I leaned down a little until I could see them both through the open window. "Can I help you gentlemen?"

Blondie glanced over at the driver, a hefty man with a head full of black hair slicked back like a young Elvis. His body was Older Elvis. Elvis gave a nod to Blondie and opened the driver-side door. Blondie followed suit, unfolding his lanky frame from the car and standing directly in front of me on the sidewalk.

"Yeah, we gotta message for ya," Elvis said, walking around me until he was beside his buddy." There was nothing about the voice that remotely hinted of having roots south of the Mason-Dixon Line.

Both wore sunglasses and were decked out in casual trousers, bright print Hawaiian-style shirts, and polished leather shoes. Their clothing might've passed for touristy wear in Miami Beach, but here in the Panhandle it was almost laughable. The King looked around my age, Blondie a few years younger despite the retreating hairline.

"What's the message?" I said, eyeballing one, then the other.

Elvis glanced around at the surroundings while the blond beanpole kept his eyes locked on me. The King turned around slowly until a pistol stuffed in the back of his trousers grabbed my attention. "Lay off," he said, turning back to face me.

"Lay off? Of what?"

"Don't play dumb," Blondie growled, his voice deeper than his stout cohort's. I guess it had farther to travel up and out. "We know who sent you."

"Oh, yeah? And just who would that be?" I didn't have a clue what they were talking about but decided to play along. I hoped they couldn't see the nervousness I was doing my damnedest to keep at bay. If they'd tailed me to Canal Park and had seen me talking with Bo Pickron, that might be enough to keep them in check, for the moment, anyway. Still,

I wished to hell I had my shotgun in hand. I made a mental note to reconsider buying a handgun.

Elvis reached into his shirt pocket, pulled out a comb, and ran it through his hair a couple of times, then put it back. My gut tightened, but I tried not to let my eyes show anything. That comb and the one I'd found near my burned trailer were identical twins. "I'm gonna say this one more time," he said, giving me a stare that even through the shades felt as icy as a cold north wind. "Back off. And tell your boss we're onto him. Tell him shit sometimes runs uphill."

And just like that, they climbed back in the fancy wheels and drove away.

Back in St. George I took a chance and called the police department. I recognized Beth's voice on the other end of the line.

"Is Patrolman Owens on duty today?" I said, trying to disguise my voice.

"Yes, sir, but he's out right now. I can patch you through if you like."

I declined Beth's offer. The last thing I needed was for her or Ben Merritt overhearing J.D. and me talking.

St. George isn't that big of a place, maybe three miles of highway along the beach from city limit to city limit, but it took damn near an hour of riding around before I spotted J.D.'s blue-and-white a block off the beach on Seventh Street near The Green Parrot. He had pulled over an older-model Toyota and was talking through the window to a young brunette. I slowed down to make sure Ben Merritt wasn't with him and then pulled to the side of the road behind his cruiser to wait for him to finish the traffic stop.

He looked back at me and held up a finger, either shooting me the bird or signaling he'd be a minute, and continued the conversation with the brunette. Another few seconds passed, then J.D. leaned into the open window, and he and the girl kissed.

I grinned as he approached my truck. "Taking bribes from the public already?"

His face flushed. "No, sir, that was my girlfriend. You didn't see that, okay?"

"See what?"

He blew out a breath. "Thanks."

"Your boss man around?"

"No, sir. He comes on at four, then I'm back on at midnight."

I'd noticed the conspicuous lack of policemen since I'd been in St. George. "Aren't you guys a little short-handed?"

J.D. glanced toward the highway, looking east to west. "Yes, sir. A couple of men up and quit in the spring. Couldn't get along with the chief, is what I heard. That's when I hired on. I heard some talk we're supposed to be getting somebody else soon, though. The chief likes to run a tight ship, if you know what I mean."

"Yeah, I know the type."

"The County sends a car over now and then when we need a break," J.D. said.

I nodded, remembering that I'd seen a green-and-white cruising the streets of St. George on a few occasions.

J.D. looked down, shuffling his feet. "I been keeping my eyes and ears open like you said."

"And?"

"I heard Chief Merritt on the phone once. I think he was talking to somebody at Barfield's. I also seen him with Clayton Barfield, Brett's daddy. They were talking out in the parking lot back of the station, but I couldn't make out anything they said."

I nodded. "Good, keep it up, but be careful." I looked around. "Have you ever heard Chief Merritt talking to anybody from up north, or hear him mention anything about somebody from up there?" What the hell, it was worth a shot.

"Up north? You mean like Yankees?"

"Yeah."

J.D. mulled it over a minute. "No, sir, not that I can think of, except maybe tourists down here on vacation. Nothing official-like, though."

I nodded. "Is there anywhere we can go where we won't be seen? I've got something I think you'll be interested in seeing."

J.D. thought for a moment. "Yes, sir, my daddy's place. Him and Mama are on vacation up at Lake Martin. We can park in the garage, and I got a key to the house. You follow me, but keep back a block or so, just in case."

I followed J.D. for several blocks through an older residential area of St. George about a half-mile inland from the beach. He pulled into a weathered concrete driveway, got out, and swung open the doors of a detached wood-framed garage. I drove in and parked beside his cruiser, then followed him out a side door to the back of the house. He unlocked the door, and we stepped into the kitchen. It was an older home but clean and well-maintained.

"You want a Coke or something?" J.D. said, opening the refrigerator and grabbing a bottle.

"No thanks." I pulled a chair away from the table and sat down. He sat across from me, and I slid the manila envelope to him. "Take a gander at these."

J.D. slugged down about a third of his Coke and began looking through the stack of 8×12s. He gave a low whistle. "Where'd you get these?"

"From Tom Mayo's widow. She said Tom had been conducting his own investigation because Ben Merritt kept interfering when he tried doing his job."

Another whistle. "The mayor's wife and Lamar Randall?"

I took the photos back when J.D. finished gawking at them. "So, we have Chief Merritt sitting in Mayor Harper's car," I said. "We have Chief Merritt and Brett Barfield together. Lamar and the mayor's wife. Lamar and Brett. And you saw Merritt and Clayton Barfield talking behind the station."

J.D. drained the last of his Coke. "Why do you think Coach Mayo would've took that picture of the Barfields' fishing boat?"

I spent the next few minutes filling J.D. in on what I'd found out for sure, my theory about Clayton Barfield using his fleet of boats to smuggle drugs, and how Ben Merritt might be in on the deal by looking the other way and keeping Brett Barfield out of trouble.

"But why would the mayor have been in on it? Them two families don't like each other—except for Brett and Maddie, I mean."

"Mayor Harper stood to lose most of his wealth to Maddie once she turned twenty-one and inherited what her father left her," I said. "George Harper might've been counting on his cut of the drug money as a hedge against that."

J.D. looked confused. "Call it a retirement fund. And, there's something else." I pulled out my wallet and handed J.D. the newspaper photo of Brett. "Look at this real good and tell me who it reminds you of."

J.D. gave the clipping a quick glance and shrugged. "It's Brett Barfield. That's his senior picture."

I nodded. "But look again. The shape of the face, that cleft in his chin. You've seen the Harper Realty billboards around town. Friendly George?"

J.D. looked from the clipping to me, his eyes wide. "Wait a minute, are you saying . . . ?"

"George Harper was Brett's biological father. Sheriff Pickron admitted it after I'd figured it out. You do know Bo Pickron is Mrs. Harper's brother, don't you?"

"Yes, sir."

"George Harper and Brett's mother used to date back in high school. They had an affair years ago, after they were both married. My guess is the honorable mayor was paying Chief Merritt to keep Brett out of hot water, and when Tom Mayo busted Brett with the marijuana, Merritt made sure the charges didn't stick. It wound up costing Mayo his job and maybe his life."

After emphasizing just how dangerous this whole mess might get if word leaked out, I swore J.D. to secrecy and left. I hoped I could trust him. I'd counted on men younger than him to cover my back in more dangerous situations, but they were highly trained Marines. If this young police officer couldn't keep his mouth shut, I might wind up in a real world of hurt. Or worse.

I jolted awake. Was I dreaming, or was somebody knocking on my door? I leaned over to the nightstand and squinted at the clock. It was a little after midnight, and I was still groggy from a few too many beers. Another knock. Thinking it might be Kate or Jerry and Donna needing help, I switched on a light and hurried to the door without checking out the window first. Big mistake. I opened the door to face a pistol clutched in the meaty fist of Elvis.

Elvis and Blondie barreled their way in without invitation, Blondie greeting me with a short but effective punch to the solar plexus. I dropped to my knees, gasping for air.

Elvis grabbed me by the hair and jerked my head up until I was staring him in the face. "I don't think we got our point across in town this aftanoon, friend," he said and then slammed me upside the head with the gun butt. "Lay off!"

Friend? I thought, as the world spun and the light faded. *With friends like these . . .*

CHAPTER 20

Kate checked the schedule at work and called the next morning to let me know Lamar was supposed to have the coming Tuesday off. She also found out from Tonya Randall that her mother was still working the four-to-midnight shift at the hospital. She didn't press her luck and try to find out what day or days Debra Randall had off from her nursing duties.

I didn't bother telling Kate about my little run-in with the goons from up north. I was nursing a headache, and Elvis's blow had raised a nice goose egg, but surprisingly there was little bleeding. I guess being thick-skulled has its virtues.

I did call Bo Pickron to tell him about yesterday's afternoon chat and late-night visit with my two new "friends." He seemed duly unimpressed.

"Look, Sheriff, those guys were in a rental car, and their accent tells me they're from somewhere up north. This thing is obviously more than a local deal. Maybe it's time you called in the State or the Feds."

"No can do, McClellan, unless you got some hard evidence that I can show 'em. They won't lift a finger on a whim." I thought about the comb I'd found near my burned trailer and mentally kicked myself in the ass for throwing it away.

Pickron did promise to have his men keep an eye out for the car, which I described for him in as much detail as I could. "Don't count on us finding it, though," he said. "Chances are they already ditched the car across the state line somewhere and rented another since you ID'd 'em with it."

At dusk I left the highway and turned onto the dirt road that ran through the woods parallel to the side boundary of Harper property. Checking the Google map again, I stopped where the sandy rut road made a hairpin turn south toward a cypress swamp. I pulled off and parked behind a thick clump of underbrush. Scratched the hell out my Silverado doing it, but the truck would be hard to spot if anybody happened by. I backtracked down the road until the underbrush thinned some, then worked my way through the woods and came to the white fence marking the estate boundary. I climbed over and snuck back a couple of hundred yards along the fence line until the house was in sight. Using trees and bushes for cover, I eased within thirty-five or forty yards of the house.

I made myself comfortable in a spot where I was well concealed by a hedge and had a good view of the driveway and front of Tara. The air was hot and sticky. I was wearing my camos, sleeves and neck buttoned tight because the mosquitoes were out in force, but a light breeze and bug juice spared me some discomfort.

Kate and I already had photo evidence linking Lamar Randall and Marilyn Harper, but getting up-to-date photographic proof that their affair was still ongoing since Maddie's death and Brett's disappearance might prove important to the case. I waited, hoping that if Lamar and Marilyn were feeling amorous tonight they'd do their thing early, leaving plenty of time for Lamar to beat his wife home from her shift at the hospital.

It wasn't long before I was fighting sleep. It reminded me of being on a listening post in the Marines, only there was no one else along to spare me a couple of hours of shut-eye. I had six hours watching all to myself. By eleven-thirty the only visitors to Tara were the aforementioned squadrons of mosquitoes, scattered fireflies, and a family of chattering raccoons that passed within a few feet without detecting me. I gave it up for the night and headed home.

Tuesday was Lamar's day off from Gillman's, so I was back on post by seven that morning. I knew his wife wouldn't leave for work until midafternoon, but Lamar might use some excuse to get away from the house for a while. If he did, I wanted to be ready and not blow the opportunity.

At ten I heard the sound of an engine break the calm. I grabbed the binoculars I'd borrowed from Kate and made sure my camera was at the ready. Soon a van appeared out of the trees and made a half circle around the drive. I focused the binoculars at a rectangular sign on the car door. *Adele's Cleaning Service*, then a couple of lines in smaller lettering I couldn't make out and a phone number in bold along the bottom. No Lamar, but the attractive young woman with big boobs and eggplant-colored hair who climbed out broke the boredom. I wondered if Friendly George or Marilyn had made the hire. My money was on the mayor.

Adele left around one in the afternoon. I made myself comfortable against the tree at my back and dozed off for a while. In the Corps I'd learned to be a light sleeper; if another vehicle came driving up, I'd hear it.

I was on full alert again by four, the time Debra Randall began her shift at the hospital. The hours dragged by, darkness fell, and I spent another wasted night waiting for lover boy. Not even the raccoons bothered to make a show, although a possum walked by close enough that I could've reached out and touched it.

They say the third time's a charm, and I damn sure hoped it would be. I was getting tired of spending hour after hour waiting for Lamar and Marilyn to get their hormones in gear. Back on station at five-thirty Wednesday afternoon, I didn't have long to wait. I was barely settled in when I heard a vehicle's engine in the distance and getting closer by the second. I readied the binoculars and camera. Bingo!

It was Lamar's old pickup, all right; the camouflage paint job was unmistakable. Instead of turning off for the garage, he parked in the circular drive. I grabbed the camera, zoomed in, and snapped a few pictures as he climbed out of the truck and headed for the door. The lighting was good, and I had the camera set on silent mode so he couldn't hear the shutter clicking.

Lamar ambled up the steps and across the porch. I kept shooting as he rang the doorbell. A minute passed, and he rang it again. A few

seconds later the door flew open. Lamar stepped back and nearly stumbled as Marilyn Harper came at him like a she-tiger, screaming at the
top of her lungs, arms flailing and fists pounding Lamar's head and
chest as he retreated down the steps. I snapped shot after shot as she
reached in a pocket of her robe and threw something at him, all the
while screaming like a banshee. Her voice was so shrill and choked with
sobs I couldn't make out what she was saying.

Except for one specific word, a word she repeated three or four
times during the brief tirade—"Maddie!"

"Dang, Mac, that *is* money! Look closer, right there." Kate tapped the
nail of her pinky on the screen. "Those are bills."

I'd driven straight to Kate's house when I left the woods, and she
uploaded the photos from my camera to her laptop. The pics were
pretty good as they were, but the Picasa program was bringing out even
better detail.

Kate's eyes searched mine. "Money. What on earth do you think
it means?"

I looked again at Lamar, bent over, scooping up the bills that had
spilled from the envelope Marilyn hurled at him. "I don't know, but I
doubt it's a past-due stud fee. I could use a beer."

I followed Kate into the kitchen and collapsed onto a chair. The
surprise of watching Marilyn Harper attacking Lamar had knocked me
for a mental loop. Or maybe the long hours I'd spent sitting and spying
the past three days had caught up with me.

Kate handed me a beer and twisted the top off her own. She went
back to the living room and returned with her laptop. "You're sure you
heard her say 'Maddie'?"

"Three or four times, and loud enough to scare the bark off the trees."

Kate scrolled through a few more photos, each one a little more
blurry than the preceding shots. "You were shaking the camera on
these."

I took a big swig. "Well, excuse me. I was expecting to see them act all lovey-dovey, and then she comes at him like a mama bear screaming Maddie's name."

She ignored my explanation. "We need to find out what the money was for."

I resisted the urge to say, "No shit" and grabbed the stack of 8×12s instead. I found the ones with Lamar Randall and Marilyn Harper together and set them side-by-side. Then I found the one showing Lamar and Brett beside a pickup truck and added it to the lineup. "Scroll back to the clear shots I took this evening," I said.

When Kate was ready I pointed to the photos of Lamar and Marilyn acting like love-struck teenagers inside the Continental. "Okay. Here, those two are love birds. And here," I said, pointing to the ones showing Lamar walking from the Harpers' garage to Marilyn waiting at the front door, "I'd guess they were fixing to get it on again while Friendly George was away."

I picked up the shot of Lamar and Brett, where the camera had captured what appeared to be an argument of some kind. "Looks to me like Lamar is threatening Brett here, or at least they're having a dis-agreement over something. What do you think?"

Kate picked up the photo and examined it again. "I agree, but what about?"

"Who does Marilyn Harper despise most in this world?"

Kate thought a moment. "Nora Barfield . . . and Brett."

I took another swig of beer. "I think Marilyn was getting Lamar to lean on Brett, probably to get him and Maddie to stop seeing each other."

Kate's eyes widened. "She was paying him to break them up?"

"That's my guess, but not with money. Lamar had been carrying a torch for Mare for years. She knew it, and started romancing Lamar to persuade him to be her lap dog."

Kate took a sip of beer and lightly massaged her forehead. "But where does the money fit in, and all that anger toward Lamar?"

"Okay, think back. When did Lamar hurt his eye?"

"A couple of months ago, I think."

"Around the same time that Brett and Maddie supposedly eloped, wasn't it?"

Kate took a deep breath and let it out slowly. "Yeah, it was. Wait, you don't think—"

The Marines' Hymn cut off Kate's words. I grabbed the cell phone and answered.

"McClellan?" It was Sheriff Bo Pickron.

"Go."

"I need to see you this evening."

"What for?"

"Brett Barfield turned up this afternoon."

Barfield? This could answer a lot of questions. "Where?"

"In the national forest, at the bottom of a sinkhole. Dead."

CHAPTER 21

That evening at dusk I was on my way to Parkersville to see Sheriff Pickron when an older-model white Ford sedan pulled onto the highway just in front of me about a block from Canal Park. I had to hit the brakes, even though I was observing the seasonal city speed limit of 35 mph. The driver's head barely cleared the top of the seat. He was wearing a straw fedora like many of the older male tourists in these parts, but with my headlights practically on his bumper I noticed right away the car bore a Florida license plate.

I muttered a few choice words and backed off. Just outside the city limits he sped up gradually, but he was still doing well under the posted limit of 60. I closed the gap a couple of times as an incentive for him to speed up, but each time the old geezer tapped his brakes.

It was after what passed for rush hour around the St. George-Parkersville metropolis area, and there was very little traffic, but I didn't want to risk passing yet because there always seemed to be some fool driving without lights in this twilight between day and night. The highway between the two towns passed through a few miles of paper company land planted in slash pines, which made visibility that much poorer. A long stretch of straight highway was coming up in another half mile, so I decided to play it safe and wait.

The road finally straightened out. I eased over near the center line and squinted past the slow-moving Ford ahead. Satisfied it was clear, I turned on my left blinker and pulled into the other lane. Damned if the car didn't speed up when I did, not an uncommon occurrence with some assholes who think they own the road. I gave the Silverado a little more gas and then floored it. Just as the passing gear kicked in, the passenger-side window exploded, peppering my right cheek with glass shards and blasting a hole through the driver-side window.

At first I didn't know what the hell had happened, but when the second round buzzed past my head and took out the rest of my window I pretty much had it figured out. I ducked as low as I could while still maintaining control and cut the wheel left, at the same time lifting off the gas and braking as quickly as I dared. The truck ran off the shoulder of the road, jolted across a shallow grassy ditch, and plowed into the forest. Luckily, the Silverado came to rest between two rows of pines planted just far enough apart to accommodate it.

Keeping low, I grabbed the shotgun off the floorboard where I'd kept it whenever driving since the goons from up north had made their late-night visit. I jacked a shell into the chamber, then slipped the transmission into park, killed the engine, and pulled the key out of the ignition. I left the headlights shining into the woods, hoping the ambushers would think I was injured or dead. Reaching up, I flicked the dome light switch to "off" so it wouldn't come on automatically. I unbuckled my seat belt, then, easing the door open just enough to get the job done, I slipped outside.

I crawled to the back tire. Using it as a shield, I peeked under the truck bed. Down the road, headlights flashed in a half circle and headed back my way, then went out. I heard the Ford swishing through the high grass growing in the shallow ditch. I kept my eyes away from the glow of the taillights and hoped like hell my eyes would adjust to the darkness in time. The Ford's motor died; a car door creaked open and then closed with little noise. Whoever it was had been wise enough to turn off their interior light, too.

I took some deep breaths and let my ears do the work while my eyes got better adjusted to the dark. I was in combat mode now, and I felt that rush I'd experienced during my tours in Iraq. A minute or so passed, then I heard footsteps, barely audible but coming my way. All those long nights on watch as a Marine were paying off.

A hulking shadow with pistol drawn approached the truck and

crept toward the passenger-side door. I eased into a catcher's squat, shotgun at the ready, safety off. Damned if I was going to give the shooter another crack at me. When he was just a few paces from the truck I bolted up, point-aimed the scattergun, and squeezed the trigger, no questions asked. The Maverick roared and bucked, and in the muzzle blast I saw the dark figure tumble backward. I chambered a round, ready in case another shooter might be approaching. Instead, I heard the Ford start up, and then the squeal of tires on pavement as it sped back toward St. George.

I waited a moment, then crept around to the other side of the truck. The shooter lay sprawled on the forest floor, arms outstretched above his head like he was reaching for Heaven. He wasn't moving, but I kept the barrel trained on him as I approached to check for a pulse. I gave the body a light kick in the ribs, then bent down and placed my fingertips on his neck. Nothing.

I tried to feel something inside, but all I came up with was numb. This wasn't the first life I'd taken, but after Fallujah I'd hoped to never face this kind of situation again. But life is that way. We don't always get what we hope for.

And there was no mistaking who it was lying at my feet. The King was dead.

While I caught my breath a few vehicles passed by in either direction, but I had already doused the truck lights and was far enough off the road and in the woods that none of them even slowed.

I figured Blondie must've been driving, wearing the hat and slumped low in the seat while Elvis had kept out of sight in the back. But how the hell had they tailed me from Kate's house? Then it struck me. Somebody, and my money was on Merritt, must've known I was there and somehow tipped them off that I was heading out on Highway 98. The no-good bastard.

When I'd calmed down enough, I called Pickron on his cell phone and told him where I was and what had happened. He came out right away by himself, listened to my spiel, and checked out the scene.

Long story short: Bocephus warned me not to mention a word to anybody about what had gone down. His department would keep things under wraps as long as possible while they ran a make on the guy. Meanwhile, if any reporters came snooping around, a John Doe had been found in the woods, cause of death as of yet undetermined.

Not a problem. I sure as hell didn't want Kate knowing how close I'd come to buying the farm. Luckily, there were no bullet holes or other damage to my Silverado that I could see, other than the shattered glass. A vandal or would-be thief had busted out the windows while my truck was parked on the street during my meeting with the sheriff, and I'd nicked myself in a couple of places while shaving above my beard.

I figured Kate would buy it, especially if I kept busy for a couple of days getting the glass replaced and giving my peppered cheek time to heal before seeing her again.

Before he left, Pickron filled me in on what he knew about Brett Barfield's untimely demise. A group of archaeological students from FSU had been exploring sinkholes for artifacts and other evidence of Native American culture in an area of the national forest only a couple of miles from the Grand Gator Bay Wilderness Area. Rappelling to a wide ledge in one sinkhole that led to a cavern, a student had spotted a body floating in the water twenty feet below. The U.S. Forest Service and local sheriff's department were called in and the body recovered. Brett's wallet was still in his pocket, his ID, a few dollars in cash, and credit cards intact.

So much for my theory that Brett Barfield was alive and on the lam.

Pickron's parting words: "Watch your ass, McClellan. I doubt this character will hang around, but you never know."

A week later, the autopsy results revealed that Brett Barfield had suffered a gunshot wound to the abdomen at point-blank range. The bullet had passed through the body and wasn't recovered. His lungs contained fresh water, indicating the wound had not been instantly fatal. A rope was found around the body. Someone had shot Brett, tied a rock or some other weight to his body, and dumped him into the sinkhole. Somehow over time, the weight had worked loose and the body floated to the surface. Though the medical examiner estimated Brett had been dead two to three months, the body was in much better condition than Maddie's due to the cold, mineral-laden water and lack of scavengers.

More telling, limestone samples taken from the sinkhole matched those found imbedded in the scalp of Madison Lynn Harper. It was likely that Maddie had met her fate in the same location.

Kate had been right all along; Clayton Barfield and Chief Ben Merritt had been arguing, not laughing, the night we'd seen them in the alley beside the bank in Parkersville. That was evident at Brett's funeral. Clayton seemed as distraught as his wife, Nora, and something told me it was no act.

Damn fine detective I was turning out to be.

CHAPTER 22

"D on't you think you should let Bo Pickron in on what we've learned?" Kate said, snuggling closer. She'd come over after work Friday for grilled trout and vegetables. One thing led to another, and now we were lying in bed, staring out the window at the myriad of stars visible through the pine tops.

I let out a deep breath, being careful not to trip up and let slip anything about the shooting incident. There had been no trace of Blondie around the area the past few days, and I was beginning to breathe a little easier. "Maybe, but we can't prove anything except that his sister and Lamar were probably having an affair. I doubt if he'll be overjoyed to hear that. And the rest is just our theory."

"But it all makes sense," Kate said. "Lamar injures his eye around the same time Maddie and Brett disappear; the photos Tom Mayo took showing they were lovers; and yours, showing Marilyn attacking Lamar and throwing an envelope full of money at him while screaming Maddie's name."

"That money could've been for anything. Maybe Lamar did some work for her and she wasn't satisfied with the results."

Kate propped up on an elbow and stared at me. "Dang, Mac, you can be so stubborn sometimes. What *do* we need, then?"

"Let's see . . . a motive wouldn't hurt, and the weapon whoever shot Brett with would add a nice touch."

Kate gave my shoulder a shove, then snuggled close again and draped an arm across my chest. "I'm going to sleep. Some of us have to get to work early."

I lay there for a long time, feeling Kate's warm body nestled against mine, listening to the sound of her soft breathing. I recalled her words, "Some of us have to get to work early."

I was one of them.

The next morning I was up in time to cook Kate breakfast. As soon as she left for work I began rehearsing just how I would approach Marilyn Harper and what I'd say when I paid her an unexpected visit. I was heading out the door when my phone rang. I sat on the picnic bench and punched the talk button. "McClellan."

"It's J.D. Owens, sir. You got a minute?"

"Sure, what's up?"

"I was in Chief Merritt's office this morning right after my shift ended when he got a call," J.D. said, talking faster than usual. "Soon as he answered he told me to get lost, so I went to the lobby. Beth asked me to watch the desk for her while she went to the bathroom, so I told her I would."

"Slow down, J.D., I can hardly make out what you're saying."

"Yes, sir, sorry. Anyway, Beth usually takes her time when she uses the bathroom. I don't know what all she does in there, but—"

"Get to the point, J.D. This isn't about Beth using the bathroom, is it?"

"No, sir. So, I'm sitting in her chair, and I get to thinking about what you said, about keeping my ears open and all. Anyway, I picked up the phone quiet as I could and listened in on what the chief was saying."

There was a pause. "What did you hear?"

"He was talking to Clayton Barfield. Mr. Barfield said something about a boat coming in, and going floundering tonight, after midnight I think he said, but I'm not real sure. What do you reckon he meant by that?"

"Floundering? I don't know. Anything else?"

"The chief said something about him taking care of it. Don't know what he meant by that, either. I was starting to get scared by then, thinking I might get caught, so I hung up. Good thing, too. Beth come out of the bathroom about two seconds later."

"That's good work, J.D.," I said, "but don't go taking chances like that again. We don't need you getting your butt in a sling with Merritt."

Had J.D. Owens stumbled onto something important? Why the hell would Clayton Barfield advise Ben Merritt he planned to go floundering after midnight? What business was it of Merritt's, and what was it that Merritt would take care of? My gut told me the chief wasn't the least bit interested in buying any fresh flounder from Barfield Fisheries.

Then the proverbial lightbulb switched on in my head. Damn, sometimes two plus two really does equal four. I'd deal with the floundering issue later, but right then I had another fish to grill. I drove to the Harper property and turned onto the winding drive toward Tara. I parked just past the front porch and grabbed the manila envelope off the seat. To my surprise Marilyn Harper opened the door after the first ring.

"Morning, Mare." It was only nine-thirty, but she was already slurping down the martinis. She was wearing a white bathrobe with matching slippers and looked like she'd aged ten years since my previous visit.

Her eyes narrowed and she leaned her face closer to me like she was trying to focus. "Do I know you?"

Her breath was sour, and I tried not to flinch. "Yes, ma'am, I'm Mac McClellan. We spoke here a while back."

She weaved and stumbled back a step before catching her balance. "Oh, sure, Mac. You make the best martinis. Come on in.

"Excuse the mess," she said, waving her free hand above her head as I followed her into the great room. "The cleaning wench comes twice a week, but things have been a mess lately."

Wench? Adele must've been Friendly George's idea after all. "Looks fine to me," I said. And it did. From the looks of things, Adele was a worthwhile hire. Except for several martini glasses scattered about and an overturned pitcher lying next to a red purse on the bar, the house was spic and span.

Marilyn swayed to the bar and topped off her glass from a half-empty pitcher. "So Mac, what brings you here this fine morning?"

No sense beating around the bush when it seemed the booze had loosened Marilyn's tongue and fogged her memory of our previous meeting. "I'm trying to find out who's responsible for Maddie's death, and I believe you can help me."

Marilyn's knees almost buckled as she took a step toward me. She turned and leaned against the bar. "Brett Barfield killed my Maddie. Drowned her when he crashed that damned boat of his." Then she laughed. "That bastard got his, though. Son of a bitch is dead! Left my Maddie to drown, but now the sorry bastard is finally dead, too!"

She was spitting venom, and her face looked like evil incarnate. I was treading a fine line here, like tiptoeing through a mine field. "Lamar Randall killed Brett Barfield, didn't he, Mare?"

She started like she'd been slapped, and what little color was left in her already pasty face drained away. "No, he . . . it was some drug dealer the bastard was trying to double-cross."

"You were paying Lamar to get him to break up Maddie and Brett, weren't you?"

She flung the glass at me. It sailed over my head and crashed against a wall in the great room. "How dare you come into my house and accuse—"

"I've got photos of you and Lamar together," I said, holding up the envelope. "Photos your brother would be very interested in seeing."

She weaved again and grabbed the bar to keep from falling. She steadied herself, then took a clean glass from a row on the bar and poured another drink. Somehow she managed to scoot up on one of the plush, high-backed barstools. "You're bluffing," she spat. "You don't know a goddamn thing."

I pulled out the shot Tom Mayo had taken of the love birds kissing in the Lincoln. "So, call my hand."

She leaned forward and squinted at the photo. I stepped closer and held it a foot away from her face so she wouldn't topple off the stool. She grimaced, her lips nearly disappearing. "You don't know anything. He needed a ride one day and he kissed me, that's all."

I slipped the other shot of the two in the car from the envelope and showed it to her. I followed that up with Mayo's photos of her waiting for Lamar at the front door. "Nice of you to let your guests park in your garage while they visit. Or maybe you didn't want to risk anyone seeing Lamar's vehicle at your house while the mayor was away."

I showed her the in-focus shots I'd taken of her attacking Lamar and throwing the money at him. "And I suppose this was payment for an odd job? I heard you screaming Maddie's name while I took these."

Marilyn gulped down the rest of her martini, swiveled in the stool, and grabbed the pitcher to pour another. She smiled, or was it a sneer? "Those photographs don't prove a goddamn thing, and you still don't know anything."

"I know your husband was Brett Barfield's biological father," I said, watching for Marilyn's reaction to my ace-in-the-hole bluff, "and I also know your husband was paying bribe money to Chief Merritt to keep Brett out of trouble." I waited, but all Marilyn did was to keep the smiling sneer plastered on her face and begin pumping a foot up and down on the stool's foot rest.

"You hated Brett Barfield because you knew he was your husband's illegitimate son. And you hated him because he and Maddie fell in love and planned to get married. Brett and Maddie were first cousins, and you couldn't stand the thought of Brett touching her. You hated that Maddie was carrying Brett's child. You hated the thought of them being together so much that you paid Lamar Randall to do whatever it took to make sure they didn't stay together.

"Only something went wrong, didn't it?" I said, noticing Marilyn's chin begin to quiver and her foot flail faster. "Terribly wrong. Lamar met Brett out in the middle of nowhere to make him a final offer to stay away from Maddie. But Brett wasn't buying, so Lamar pulled out a gun to scare him, and the two started fighting.

"Lamar didn't know it, but Maddie was there with Brett. And when she saw Lamar pull the pistol, and he and Brett struggling over it, Maddie came running and nearly scratched Lamar's eye out to try to stop him from hurting the man she loved.

"Lamar shoved her away, and that's when poor Maddie fell into the sinkhole. Lamar and Brett kept fighting until the gun went off. Brett slumped to the ground, shot through the gut. Lamar panicked. He'd only meant to scare Brett from seeing Maddie anymore, and now two people were dead. Then he weighted Brett's body with a rock and dumped it into the same—"

"Shut up! Shut up, you son of a bitch!"

I'd been too caught up imagining the scene to notice Marilyn reach into her purse and pull out a snub-nosed revolver. She held the pistol in one hand, the martini glass in the other. Both were shaking. Gin sloshed out of the glass; I hoped a bullet wouldn't spill from the barrel pointed at my chest.

"You forced your way in here and tried to rape me, Mac," Marilyn slurred. "Too bad I had to shoot you. Who's the sheriff going to believe, his own sister or some newcomer who broke in and attacked her?"

I stared into Marilyn's eyes. I'd seen that look before. She meant business, and there was no time to lose. I flung the envelope at her and darted to the left just as she jerked the trigger and the revolver barked. The recoil sent her gun hand flying into her face, knocking her back against the bar and onto the floor. In a flash I pinned her arm with one hand and grabbed the revolver with the other. I stood and looked down. Her martini hand was clasped over her nose, blood pouring through her fingers. She was shuddering and crying out Maddie's name between labored breaths. The woman had just tried to kill me, but I couldn't help feeling sorry for her.

I slipped the revolver inside my free back pocket, grabbed a couple of folded cloth napkins from a stack on the bar, and dropped them beside her face. She took the napkins and wadded them against her nose, still sobbing as I picked up the envelope and left.

I brushed by the secretary, stormed into Bo Pickron's office, and slapped Marilyn's pistol and the manila envelope on his desk. "Your sister just tried to kill me, Pickron. I don't want to press charges, but the woman needs some serious help."

For the first time since I'd met him, Sheriff Bocephus Pickron was speechless. His face paled as he reached for the revolver.

"Careful, it's still loaded."

He thumbed open the cylinder latch and dumped the spent cartridge and four remaining rounds into his palm.

"My prints are on it, too. I was too worried about getting my ass shot off to be dainty when I took it from her."

Pickron stared at the revolver, holding it at different angles to the light. "It's Marilyn's. Was she drinking?"

"Does she ever stop?"

Pickron looked like he'd had the wind knocked out of his sails. "It's been a long time since I've seen her anywhere close to sober." He laid the weapon aside and reached for the envelope. "What's this?"

"Photos. Tom Mayo took the black and whites, I took the colored shots. I've got copies so I'm leaving these with you. Let me know what you think, if you're interested."

Pickron picked up the envelope with both hands and tapped it on the desktop a couple of times like he was lost in thought.

"I need to know something, Pickron. Did you tell your sister about Maddie's autopsy, that she didn't die in the bay?"

He stared past me and nodded. "Yeah, after George's funeral. She kept putting him down, blaming him for what happened to Maddie. George was a lot of things, McClellan, but he was no murderer. Marilyn needed to know that."

"You should've told her sooner. Harper might still be alive."

Pickron flinched like I'd jabbed him in the jaw. "What do you mean?"

"Just check out the photos."

He grunted, his way of saying he'd get around to it.

"Anything on Elvis yet?"

Pickron looked confused.

"The guy I took down."

He shook his head. "When we do, you'll be the first to know. All the ID on the body was fake, like we figured. Pistol's untraceable. We're running the prints and dentals. We did find the stolen car they used abandoned in Georgia, so it looks like his partner's flown the coop."

I turned to leave. "Oh, I almost forgot. One of my sources overheard a conversation between Clayton Barfield and Ben Merritt this morning. I've got reason to believe a Barfield boat is coming in around midnight tonight. My guess is, it's carrying drugs. Merritt said something about 'taking care of it.' I plan to be there. There's your heads' up."

Pickron covered his face with both hands and let out a heavy sigh. "You got any proof?"

"No, just a hunch."

"We need solid proof. They'll never let you inside the gate without a warrant, and no judge in his right mind will issue one on hearsay."

"I'll swim."

The sheriff shoved away from the desk and rocked back in his chair. "Look, McClellan, you might not think so, but I'm on your side here. But if you go trespassing on private property like that without a warrant, you're fired."

"So fire me."

I headed for the door, then stopped and turned. "And get your sister some help."

CHAPTER 23

"Dang you, Mac, don't do it," Kate said, "it's too dangerous. Please, let the law handle it."

I laughed. "This has been going on for years, Kate. And the law is in on it, at least the law in St. George. I'm not sure where Bo Pickron stands, but he knows what's going down tonight."

I had called Kate at home after work and told her about my run-in with the Widow Harper and of my plan to sneak into Barfield Fisheries around midnight to try to get some solid proof of the smuggling operation. She'd driven right over and spent the next thirty minutes trying her best to talk me out of it.

"What can I say to make you change your mind?" she said, sniffling and on the verge of tears. "I don't want to lose you."

"You're not going to lose me. I'll be fine."

Kate held up two envelopes, letters I'd written and addressed to Megan and Mike just in case things didn't go my way. "Then what about these?" She slapped them against the kitchen table. Tears were streaking her cheeks. "I'm just supposed to send these to your kids out of the blue, letting them know their father is dead? Dang you, Mac, that's not fair to them and it sure as hell isn't fair to me!"

I moved closer, put my arm around Kate's shoulder, and kissed her salty cheek. "Look, I'll be in and out of there in no time. I'll be wearing black, I'll be camouflaged, and nobody there will be expecting anyone to show up by swimming under the security fence. Piece of cake. Quit worrying."

Kate sobbed and buried her face against my chest. "If anything happens to you, I don't know what I'll do. I lost someone before, and I don't know if I can handle that again."

This was news I hadn't heard before. I put my other arm around her and hugged her tight. "Who, Kate? Who did you lose?"

She sniffled and wiped at the tears with her fingers. "My boyfriend, over ten years ago. We had talked about getting engaged soon, just before he went fishing in the gulf with a couple of good friends. A sudden squall came up, and their boat capsized. Searchers found the boat the next day, but they never found any trace of the men. It nearly killed me, Mac. I haven't let myself get close to anyone since, until now. I don't ever want to go through that again."

Damned if this woman didn't have a tight grip on my heart-strings. I was tempted to say to hell with it and just walk away from the whole mess. But Maddie's smiling face in the photo at her funeral kept flashing through my mind; so did Joyce Mayo's look of hope that someone might finally try to prove her husband had been shafted and maybe even killed over this mess. I couldn't just turn my back on them and walk away now. I was too damn close.

I grabbed a paper napkin from the holder on the table and dabbed the tears from Kate's cheeks. Cupping her chin in my palm, I turned her face to me and smiled. "How about when this is all over you take some time off from work, and we hook up the camper and go for a little vacation? I know a couple of kids up in North Carolina who would love to meet you."

Kate managed a smile and nodded. "I'd like that. You really think they'll like me?"

I kissed her forehead. "What's not to like? You're the real deal, Just Kate Bell."

At eleven I started Kate's Honda and headed east on Highway 98. We'd agreed that using her car would give me a better chance of not being spotted, since Ben Merritt and others were familiar with my Silverado pickup. Also, with my truck parked at the campground and Kate being there with the lights on, it would give the appearance that I was home.

If I wasn't back by daylight, Kate was to call the sheriff's office and let Bo Pickron know that things had gone south on me.

I drove past the entrance to Barfield Fisheries and a quarter mile farther on turned right onto Five-Mile Island Causeway. There were a few pull-offs with picnic tables situated along the causeway. My plan was to park at the nearest of these, then walk the quarter mile or so back along the road until I was within sight of Barfield's. I'd work my way down to the water, put on my snorkeling gear, and swim to their docks.

I parked Kate's car to make it look as inconspicuous as possible and hid the key behind the left front tire. I grabbed my gear and backtracked down the causeway. Only two vehicles passed by, and I was hidden well off the road before their headlights could pick me up. A couple of hundred yards from Barfield's a pair of tall palms grew along the road-side. Using the twin trees as a landmark, I eased through the brush and marsh grass to the shore. I slipped off my shoes and donned the snorkeling gear. A waterproof camera would've made the job a lot easier, but I hadn't counted on swimming to get evidence when I bought the Lumix. To carry the camera, I had a net bag with a drawstring attached to my swim trunks to free up both hands, and the camera was sealed inside a waterproof bag. Double-checking to make sure the camera was secure at my hip, I frog-stepped into the water until I was deep enough to swim.

My time with Recon early in my Corps career gave me confidence that I could snoop around making as little noise and commotion as needed to pull this off. I was wearing black trunks and T-shirt, and camo paint covered any exposed skin. The KA-BAR combat knife strapped above my ankle and the cloud cover hiding the moon were an added bonus. I was ready to roll.

When I reached the outer fence I eased behind the next-to-last piling and took several minutes to gain my bearings and check out the situation. By hoisting myself up the piling a foot or so, I had a decent view of the two docks nearest me. I decided this piling would make as good a guidepost as any for my entrance and exit.

So far, Lady Luck was looking out for me. There were no guards around that I could see, though I was sure that would change later. Better yet, a flurry of activity on the outer dock told me the expected boat had docked there. The engine of the crane on the inner dock was chugging, and the boom was positioned over the outer dock. A big boat was moored to the inside of the outer dock; several crewmembers scurried about, packing fish and ice into wooden boxes and relaying them to others, who stacked the boxes on a large pallet attached to the crane's cable. When the pallet was loaded, the crane lifted and swung the load over the water between the two docks and lowered it onto the inner dock where other workers unloaded the boxes and carted them to waiting refrigerated trucks.

I was betting that security would increase once the fish had been off-loaded and a trusted skeleton crew got down to the real business at hand, so I decided to do a little reconnoitering while the docks were still buzzing with activity. I had no idea how far down the fencing reached and needed to find a safe way in and out. I couldn't chance a flashlight, and I knew it wouldn't be easy finding my way in the dark. Worst-case scenario, I carried a small pair of wire cutters in a pocket of my swim trunks.

I took some deep breaths, gripped the piling, and pushed myself a few feet below the surface. It was almost pitch-black, though I could see a diffused glow reflecting from the dock lights when I glanced up. Satisfied I was deep enough not to disturb the surface, I inverted and slowly descended. I stayed within reach of the piling and kept an arm extended in front of me as a "feeler" so I wouldn't nosedive into the bottom or some other unexpected structure.

I touched bottom just after clearing my ears. To my relief the fence ended two to three feet from the murky bottom, which I estimated to be around twelve to fourteen feet deep. I'd be able to scoot underneath the fence easily enough.

I swam a few yards laterally in both directions, making sure the clearing between the fence and bottom didn't alter enough to trap me inside in case I needed to make a hasty retreat. Satisfied with what I found, I located my guide piling and eased to the surface with as little movement as possible.

A good hour passed before the crane shut down and the crew began to leave the docks and disperse to the parking lot. With the distraction of the main crew leaving, this was a good time to make my move. I took a few deep breaths and swam down. I slipped underneath the fence, making sure the net bag didn't snag. Staying close to the bottom, I swept my lead hand back and forth until I contacted a piling of the outer dock. Exhaling slow and easy, I surfaced, being careful to keep to the inside of the piling. It was about six feet from the water's surface to the top of the dock. I glanced toward the fence, located my guide piling, and then scanned my new surroundings.

The boat was about twenty yards farther up the pier. I eased through the black water until I was alongside the stern. I propped the mask on my forehead for a better look. There had to be access ladders somewhere leading from the top of the dock down to the water. I finned my way toward the front of the pier until I found them, one on either side, located about fifteen yards past the bow of the boat. Great. If I hoped to get photos from here, I'd have to climb up one of those ladders, which would put me in full view of the unloading festivities if somebody happened to glance my way. No way that would work.

I wracked my brain for a minute and then decided to swim to the next dock where the now-silent crane sat. From there I could set the camera on telephoto, and hopefully would be able to get some decent shots. I might not even have to climb a ladder, depending on the angle once I got there. There were footsteps and voices above me, but the dock appeared to be deserted though still lighted. I could see I'd have to be careful to remain in the shadows. Backtracking well past the stern, I filled my lungs and headed down.

Again staying close to the bottom, I made it across with no problem. I located a piling, positioned myself on the backside, and surfaced. I rested a minute, making use of the time to survey my new vantage point. I was under the "T" section of the dock, the crane directly above me. It appeared to be deserted now, but I wasn't taking anything for granted.

Another hour dragged by. My skin was turning into a prune. Then, just as I'd suspected, a small crew walked down the outer dock and boarded the boat that had been off-loaded of its catch. The angle from here wasn't as good as I'd hoped. I'd have to take my chances and climb partway up a ladder to get any decent photos. Barely moving my fins, I eased toward the head of the dock. About halfway I spotted a ladder and made my way to it.

It was a good position, away from any direct lighting and with plenty of shadow for concealment. But then I discovered a new problem—guards on the pier opposite, standing near the end and shining flashlights around the water and out toward the "no trespassing" buoys about fifty yards away. From this distance I didn't notice any weapons, but that was one more thing I wasn't taking for granted. I had a much better view of the boat from here, but still not good enough. I watched the small crew and heard voices as they went about their business. They were making a lot less commotion than the larger crew that had off-loaded the fish.

I was mustering the nerve to climb a few rungs up the ladder when I noticed two men ambling down the dock toward the boat. As they passed beneath one of the dock lamps I got a decent look at the two. One was tall and lanky with dark hair; I couldn't be sure, but he looked like Clayton Barfield. And damned if the other man wasn't Chief Benjamin Merritt, in the flesh!

My adrenalin was pumping as I lifted a swim fin and planted it on the lowest rung of the ladder. Step-by-careful-step I worked my way up until I was halfway to the top. From there I had a good view of the boat and the off-loading activities. I wrapped an arm around a vertical rail of the ladder and made myself as comfortable as possible. Pulling the mask down until the strap rested around my neck, I reached down and slipped the camera out of the net and waterproof bags. I switched it on and set it to telephoto, then double-checked to be sure the flash was off; it was already set for silent mode and low light.

After a couple of minutes I was able to relax some. I was still in the shadows, and none of the workers or guards seemed to be paying attention to my dock. I was confident I could get what I needed and vamoose without being detected. So for the next few minutes I snapped shot after shot, hoping the dock lighting would be enough for the camera to do its job. I took several photos of crewmembers handing wrapped bales the size of suitcases out of the hold to others who loaded the cargo onto carts and disappeared at the shore end of the dock. I also made sure I got plenty of Merritt and Barfield, who continued to conveniently stand in the glow of a dock lamp and chat like they were at some Saturday night social.

After five or six minutes I figured I had all that I needed to prove Clayton Barfield was hauling more than fish with his fleet, and that Ben Merritt was involved up to his ears in it. I turned the camera off, clipped the lens cover back in place, and was about to slip it into the waterproof bag when I heard a creak above me. I froze, scarcely breathing. A minute passed, then another creak. Sweat popped out on my brow.

I waited another minute. Nothing. I started easing down the ladder when the unmistakable *click* of a hammer being drawn back rang in my ear. I froze again, hoping I hadn't been spotted but half expecting to be shot from behind.

"Don't move," a voice growled, "and drop the weapon."

"I'm not armed," I said, a partial lie since I had the KA-BAR strapped to my ankle. "This is a camera." Slowly, I raised the camera clutched in my right hand. As I did so, the protective bag slipped from my grasp and landed in the water.

"Higher, so I can see," the man said, leaning over the edge of the dock to get a better look.

I did what he said.

"Okay, now climb on up here, real slow and easy. Try anything funny and you won't live to see daylight."

The way I figured it, they weren't going to let me live to see daylight whether I cooperated or not. But right now I didn't have much choice. I had to think fast. He'd told me to climb up slow and easy, so that's what I did. On the way up, I repositioned the camera in my palm and used a finger from the other hand to slide open the memory card door on the bottom. Then I gave the card a quick press and it popped free. I wedged it between my index and middle fingers and slid the door shut.

"Over here," he said, motioning to his right with the pistol as I pulled myself onto the dock and stood. I took a few awkward sidesteps in the swim fins, keeping my back to the dock's edge. He was a burly, rough-looking character with a long beard and hair swept back in a ponytail. I wouldn't have been surprised to see a Harley Hog parked nearby. He held out his non-gun hand. "I'll take the camera," he said and at the same time turned his head and called out to somebody I couldn't see, "Hey, we got us a tourist over here!"

I've never been much of a poker player, but what the hell, my ass was already in the grinder. At this point I had nothing more to lose except my life. "I advise you to drop the weapon," I said, trying my damnedest to sound authoritative. "I'm Special Agent Carson, FBI. The gig's up. We've got this compound surrounded."

The man grinned. "Oh, yeah? Well, I'm John Dillinger, and that's Pretty Boy Floyd," he said with a quick glance over his shoulder at another guard approaching from the shadows.

That's when I flung the camera in his face and with one swift motion whirled, popped the memory card into my mouth, and dove for the water. The pistol barked twice as I hit the surface and disappeared beneath. I felt a sharp sting in my left bicep and knew I'd been hit. It wasn't the first time I'd been shot, and experience told me this was probably nothing more than a flesh wound. I did my best to ignore it and swam for the bottom.

I dove as though I was heading for the buoys, but when I reached bottom I hung a left and swam for the dock where the boat was being unloaded. I hadn't been able to get a good breath before I shoved the memory card in my mouth, and by the time I reached the dock my lungs were screaming. I popped to the surface underneath the dock, pulled the memory card from my mouth and grabbed some deep breaths. I took the time to reposition the mask over my face, and spit to keep my mouth as dry as possible. Then I gripped the memory card between my teeth and dove for the bottom again, this time heading for my guide piling on the outside fence. There was no way I'd be able to chance coming up for air once I reached it, but it gave me a certain amount of comfort knowing that that was my way out of this mess.

I was so intent on hauling ass away from there that I swam headlong into the fence, nearly knocking the mask loose. Only a little water leaked in, but there was no time to clear it. My lungs were already begging for air, and it took everything I had not to surface. I found the bottom of the fence, slipped underneath, and swam like hell, trying to get as far away as possible before I had to come up.

When I reached the point my lungs were burning and I thought I might black out, I pushed off the bottom, and my head and shoulders bolted above the surface. I grabbed the memory card and gasped for breath, filling my lungs over and over with dank salty air that had never tasted sweeter. I glanced over my shoulder. Somehow I'd managed to put about seventy-five yards between the fence and me.

Back at the docks flashlights were shining in all directions and people were scurrying about like worker ants. I heard the sound of outboards firing up and knew there was no time to waste. I dumped the water from the mask, put the card back in my mouth, and swam for all I was worth toward the twin palms where I'd left the road.

My luck was still holding when I reached the shallows not far from where I'd entered the water. I slipped off the fins and mask, took the memory card out of my mouth, and waded for shore. The card was fairly dry; I hoped my spit hadn't been enough to ruin the chances of retrieving the shots I'd taken.

I made it to dry ground and was searching for my shoes when a light shined behind me and a voice called out. "Hold it right there! Don't move, and get your hands up where I can see 'em."

I froze in place, dropped my gear, and raised my hands, the memory card clutched between the fingers of my left hand. Only then did I feel something wet and warm running down my arm and remembered I'd been shot. There was something vaguely familiar about the voice. I turned around real slow to face it. Someone was walking toward me a few feet from the waterline, keeping the light in my eyes. Behind him, I caught the shadowy outline of a boat beached thirty or forty yards away.

"You're trespassing, Mac. That's private property you just left."

The man with the light and familiar voice stepped a few feet closer, and then I recognized him. "Officer Reilly! Man, am I glad to see you." I started to lower my arms.

"Keep 'em raised," Dave Reilly said, none too friendly, his 9mm pistol pointed squarely at my chest.

"Look, Dave, I'm working with Sheriff Pickron. The Barfields have been using their boats to smuggle drugs into the area. Radio the sheriff, he'll back me up on this."

Reilly shook his head. "Can't do it, Mac. Chief Merritt wouldn't be pleased at all."

Damn! So Merritt and Barfield had Fish and Wildlife working with them, at least Officer Dave Reilly, loyal public servant. I felt the noose tightening. I'd stepped into deep doo-doo this time and was sinking lower with each passing second.

"Let's go," Reilly said, waving his pistol toward the boat, which, by brilliant deduction, I now assumed was his F and W Mako. "And keep the hands up."

We'd walked about halfway to the boat when a voice called out of the darkness, "Drop the gun, Reilly!"

I turned to see a tall, skinny silhouette scrambling down the embankment. Damned if it wasn't the cavalry coming to the rescue in the form of one Patrolman J.D. Owens! From the corner of my eye I saw Dave Reilly turn and swing his weapon in J.D.'s direction.

"Drop it!" J.D. yelled, just as Reilly's pistol belched flame, followed instantly by J.D.'s revolver. Somebody cried out, and both fell in a heap.

CHAPTER 24

Everything was happening in a flash, and my years of combat training took command. I rushed to Dave Reilly, grabbed the pistol he'd dropped, and assessed his wound. He'd taken J.D.'s round through the gut, left of center. It was bleeding badly, but if I could get the flow slowed down, he'd probably make it. I slipped the memory card into a pocket and tugged off my T-shirt. I wrung it out and folded it into a thick pressure bandage, then placed it over the entrance wound and pressed tight. Reilly was groaning but was still conscious. I grabbed his hand and placed it on the bandage. "Hold this as tight as you can," I said and then sprinted up the embankment where J.D. had fallen.

By the time I reached J.D. I'd put Reilly's pistol on safety and shoved it in the band of my swim trunks. J.D. had both hands clasped to his chest and was rolling back and forth. "Can't breathe," he managed to whisper. My blood ran cold. I'd seen it too many times before, Marines shot through the chest, gasping their last. I dropped down and grabbed his hands and pulled them away so I could see how bad he was hit.

Relief nearly overwhelmed me. I actually laughed, though I'm sure J.D. didn't think it was the least bit funny at the time. Reilly's bullet had struck Patrolman J.D. Owens in the upper chest just above the heart, but the bulletproof Kevlar vest had done its job. He'd catch his breath soon enough and would carry a nasty bruise and be sore for several days, but the bullet hadn't penetrated flesh or bone. "You are one lucky young man, J.D.," I said, grinning down at him.

His eyes opened wide. "You mean I'm not dying?" he managed to gasp.

"Not for a long time yet, J.D.," I said, patting his cheek, "not for a long time."

Sirens sounded in the distance, heading east on 98. Several vehicles with flashing lights pulled in and around Barfield Fisheries. A few minutes later another vehicle came barreling down the causeway toward us, lights flashing and siren wailing. I ran up the embankment to the road and waved my arms to flag it down. The vehicle pulled to the roadside and stopped, blue still flashing from the portable rooftop light. The door opened, and a tall, husky figure climbed out.

I'd never been so glad to see Sheriff Bocephus Pickron in my life.

"I thought you fired me today," I said to the sheriff as the ambulance carrying Dave Reilly wailed away.

"I did," he said, his face breaking into an actual smile. "How's the arm?"

I glanced at the bandage the EMT had wrapped my bicep with after cleaning the minor flesh wound. "Stings a little. Too bad you fired me; I could've used the insurance."

"You're lucky you didn't take one through the head," he said. "If it hadn't been for Owens there, I doubt we'd be talking right now."

I glanced over at where J.D. was sitting inside the sheriff's SUV, holding an icepack to his chest. He'd refused to be transported to the hospital for observation. "If Mr. McClellan isn't going, then neither am I," I heard him tell the responders.

"That kid saved your ass," Pickron said. "If he hadn't called us when he heard the gunshots, things might've turned out a whole lot worse."

Putting two and two together himself, J.D. had ignored Chief Merritt's instructions to spend his time patrolling the western end of St. George during his midnight shift. Merritt claimed he'd received complaints from several businesses and homeowners in that area of someone tampering with doors and windows. It wasn't the first time J.D. had been given such an order. Listening in on Merritt's and Clayton Barfield's conversation that morning had raised a red flag in his mind, so he decided he'd take it upon himself to look around Barfield Fisheries for any unusual activity.

After checking a few windows and doors on the west side, J.D. stopped by my trailer on his way to Barfield's to let me know what he was up to. When Kate told him about my plan and where I intended to park, he'd raced east. He'd just gotten near the main gate when the shots rang out. He immediately radioed the sheriff's department for backup and then took the causeway looking for me. Finding Kate's car, he'd turned back with his lights off, scanning the water and shoreline for signs that I'd made good my escape. That's when he saw Dave Reilly's flashlight and pistol pointing at me, and that's when Patrolman J.D. Owens made his bold move.

Sheriff Pickron barked an order to a nearby deputy and then turned to me. "You told me all you had was a hunch. How did you know this deal was coming down tonight?"

I grinned. "By brilliant deduction. My source overheard Barfield tell Merritt he was going floundering after midnight. An odd thing to say, don't you think? Flounder hide just under the sand. The bales were hidden under the fish and ice. I figured it had to be a code word for a shipment."

Pickron glanced toward his SUV. "This source of yours wouldn't happen to be one of St. George's finest, would it?"

I laughed. "Hell, Sheriff, you know a good undercover cop never reveals his sources."

CHAPTER 25

The next few days were a whirlwind of activity in and around St. George. I turned the memory card over to Bo Pickron. Luckily it wasn't damaged, and there was enough incriminating evidence from the photos I'd snapped to make a strong case for the prosecution.

Chief of Police Benjamin Merritt, after failing to convince sheriff's deputies he'd been on the scene to help bust up the drug smuggling operation, was arrested and taken into custody. Numerous charges were pending, including drug conspiracy and racketeering, extortion, and tampering with evidence.

Officer Dave Reilly was still hospitalized but was expected to fully recover and face charges.

Clayton and Nora Barfield were arrested, along with several other members of the Barfield clan and a number of employees. Barfield Fisheries was locked down while state and federal investigators searched the boats, trucks, facilities, and records for further evidence of drug smuggling. Initial findings leaked to the media indicated the illegal operation extended to Atlanta, Charlotte, and other cities farther north along the Eastern Seaboard.

After all the dead ends and blind curves I'd followed, it felt good to be right for a change.

A few days later, Kate was at my place for the steak dinner I owed her when the phone rang around six. It was Bo Pickron. He'd been busy rubbing elbows with the state and federal authorities, and it was the first time I'd spoken to him directly since the night of the bust after J.D. saved my bacon.

"McClellan, we finally got a make on the man you nailed. The guy's name was Dominic Paccelli, from Baltimore."

"Irish, huh?"

There was silence on the other end for a few seconds. Bocephus Pickron was one seriously humor-challenged individual. "Ever hear of the Abernathy family, McClellan?"

No bells rang. "No, should I have?"

"Abernathy and Sons; big seafood business in the Chesapeake Bay area. Been around for damn near a hundred years. Word is that Frank Abernathy made the family fortune in bootleg whiskey during Prohibition. Back in the day he had ties all along the Atlantic Seaboard. He was even rumored to've rubbed noses with the Kennedy family now and then."

I let out a whistle. "So, like father, like son, and so on."

"Yeah. They've even got a couple of lobbyists still working the Hill in DC."

"Promoting fresh, homegrown seafood over the imported stuff, I suppose?"

"That's the official line, but who knows what they're really buying with their pocket stuffing."

"And this Paccelli guy was working for the Abernathy family? Funny, he didn't strike me as being much of a lobbyist."

Pickron snorted, the closest thing to a laugh I'd heard from him except for his slipup the night of the bust. "I think he intended to stuff you with something besides money."

My turn to laugh. "Good one, Sheriff. But why the hell would the Abernathy family send a couple of goons after me?"

Pickron grunted. "My guess is, they thought you were working for somebody higher up the food chain."

"Yeah? Well, my guess is a certain local somebody around here set the hounds on me. I won't mention any names, but his initials are Benjamin Merritt."

"Most likely, either him or Clayton Barfield. Neither one's spilling the beans. They value their own hides too much to finger the higher-ups."

"Thanks for dragging me into this manure pile."

"You're welcome. Is Kate there?"

I felt my hackles rise. "Yeah, why?"

"Relax. She wasn't at work today when this went down. Let her know we arrested Lamar Randall this afternoon at Gillman's. Three counts of murder, or accessory to."

I glanced at the camper where Kate was inside preparing a salad to go with our steaks. "*Three* counts? Who?"

"I'm getting to it. My sister's still drying out at the psych ward," he said. "Once most of the shit was out of her system, she broke down and confessed that George didn't commit suicide after all. She's pretty much a basket case right now."

"But what about the autopsy and forensics report?" I checked the steaks and flipped them over. "You said everything pointed to it being a suicide."

Pickron let out a weary sigh. "It's complicated."

"I'm listening."

"Because of her hatred for Brett, Marilyn really believed he was responsible for Maddie's death. But later on, when Brett failed to show up, she started to have doubts. In her grief and drunken fog, she was convinced that George was after Maddie's money; she thought he wanted Maddie out of the picture so he could get his hands on every-thing. So, she spiked George's bourbon that evening with the Xanax. When he passed out at his desk, Randall was waiting. He put on rubber gloves, placed the pistol in George's hand, put his finger over George's, and pulled the trigger."

"Damn. So she believed *George* was responsible for Maddie's death?"

"Yeah. But after George's funeral, I told Marilyn about Maddie being moved and dumped in the bay after she was already dead. That's when she realized Randall had double-crossed her and lied about

Maddie and Brett. Randall tried to convince her it had all been a terrible accident, but Marilyn went berserk. You saw her throw the twenty-five grand at him."

"The blood money she promised him for killing George."

"Right. You had the scenario pretty much figured out, McClellan. Marilyn persuaded Randall to put the heat on Barfield to break him and Maddie up. He arranged to meet Barfield at the sinkholes with fifty grand in cash to buy him off. Barfield took the money and told Randall to thank Marilyn for the wedding gift. That's when Lamar pulled the pistol and told him to leave Maddie alone, or else.

"They fought over the pistol, Maddie came running out of hiding and jumped on Lamar's back and nearly gouged his eye out. During the struggle Maddie somehow fell into the sinkhole and landed on the ledge with a broken neck. About the same time the gun went off.

"Randall lost it. He never intended for anyone to get hurt, and now he had two bodies on his hands. He got rope out of his truck, tied a heavy rock to Barfield's body, and dumped him in the sinkhole. He couldn't leave Maddie's body on the ledge, because someone was bound to find it sooner or later. He thought about sinking her body too, but then he came up with the idea of staging a boating accident. If Maddie's body was found in the bay, and Barfield's body never turned up, people would most likely assume they both died in a tragic accident.

"So Randall tied a rope to his truck hitch, lowered himself to the ledge, and tied the rope around Maddie's body. He climbed out and pulled Maddie up. Then he wrapped her in a tarp and hid her in the back of his truck. He hid Barfield's truck, and then drove to the island after dark and dumped her body in the grass flats behind the Trade Winds."

"Let me guess. Lamar pocketed the fifty thousand and then told your sister that Brett and Maddie hightailed with it."

"Right. Later, a friend of Randall's who worked at Barfield's helped him steal Brett's boat out of a repair shed. Then Randall bashed in the hull and sunk it in The Stumps to make it look like a boating accident. That same friend followed Randall to north Georgia a few days later. They torched Brett's truck and pushed it into the ravine."

"I'm guessing Lamar knew about the rumor that Brett and Maddie had eloped to Georgia."

"Yeah, probably from his daughter. It was all over the school."

"Who's the friend that helped him?"

"Guy named Pete Marcengill. We're still looking for him."

I stirred the pan of mushrooms, onions, and peppers simmering on the grill. "So, with the notes Maddie and Brett left for their families saying they were eloping to Georgia, no one had any reason to believe otherwise, at least for a few weeks. Then I came along and found Maddie floating in the bay. And when she was ID'd by the dental records, Sara Gillman confessed to Kate that the whole thing about going to Georgia had been a ruse to throw the families off the trail while they honeymooned in the Keys."

"That's the best we've been able to come up with."

I took a swig of beer. "What's going to happen to your sister?"

"I've been in touch with George's lawyer in Tallahassee. Before you ask, the answer is yes. It's the same law firm the Barfields used to represent Brett. He's pretty sure we can plead temporary insanity. Like I said, Marilyn's a mess right now. She'll be confined to a mental ward for several months, and then probably do some time and be put on probation. A lot depends on the judge and what the shrinks have to say. We'll have to wait and see."

"And Lamar?"

Pickron grunted. "Second-degree or possible voluntary manslaughter for Maddie and Brett, but George was a murder for hire. He'll be lucky to stay off Death Row."

I let out a deep breath. "It's a damn shame any of this happened."

"He's the one who planted the marijuana on your boat, you know."

"Lamar?"

"Yeah. Randall was one of Brett Barfield's regular customers. When you found Maddie's body, he decided to use some of the Panama Red he bought from Barfield to put you on the hot seat. He planted the weed and made the anonymous call to Merritt."

"Damn, all this time I thought it was Merritt who tried to set me up."

Pickron let loose a genuine chuckle. "You had Merritt sweating bullets. He thought the big boys up north sent you down here to check on the two missing bales."

"You're kidding."

"No, think about it. Brett Barfield disappears and then you show up out of the blue and find Maddie's body close to where one of the missing bales floated ashore. Then you decide to hang around the area a while. I'm telling you, McClellan, you had Merritt and Clayton Barfield both checking their backsides. And that was probably why Merritt or Barfield called in Abernathy's boys."

No wonder Ben Merritt had done such a quick background check on me after I'd discovered Maddie's body. "So, I was supposed to be the alpha dogs' hit man, huh? That's funny."

"Yeah. Merritt's still not convinced you're clean."

I grabbed the tongs and moved the steaks to the warming rack. "How did Dave Reilly fit into this mess?"

"Simple. He was on Merritt's dole. What better way to ensure safe delivery of your haul than to make sure that your man was on patrol any time a shipment was coming?"

Kate stuck her head out the door and held up a beer. I checked mine and signaled thumbs up. "Anything else?"

"Some good news, maybe," Pickron said. "I'm recommending to the city council that J.D. Owens be awarded a medal of valor and a meritorious promotion to sergeant."

"I appreciate that, Sheriff, he damn sure deserves it." I was almost starting to like this guy.

"Of course, we're talking city here, and I'm county. But I think they'll see things my way."

More than likely. During my brief time here I'd learned that Sheriff Bocephus Pickron has a lot of pull in these parts, city and county.

"There's one more thing. I'm going to do my best to see that Tom Mayo's name and record are cleared. And George's lawyer's firm has agreed to see if Mayo's widow might be eligible for death benefits, pro bono."

"Now that *is* good news."

"By the way, I contacted the Sheriff's Department in Wakulla County. They sent a team with the Forest Service to check out the area around Little Gator Lake you told me about."

"They find anything?"

"You were right again. Barfield or somebody had been growing pot there. They found over a hundred plants."

"What about the trip wires?"

"Old road flares, not even wired to go off. Strictly for show to scare people away from the area."

"That's good. At least Barfield wasn't trying to kill anybody."

"Yeah. Hey, McClellan, you want your job back?"

"No thanks."

Later that evening Kate and I drove to the beach to walk off our steak dinner. The moon was high over the gulf, casting its shimmering light onto the water. A westerly breeze kept the early August night comfortable.

"I still can't believe it about Lamar," Kate said, holding her flip flops in one hand as the foaming surf rolled over our feet and then sucked at the sand underneath as it retreated from the beach. "Why on earth would he let that woman talk him into doing those awful things?"

"Love, money . . . who knows?"

"And Brett; he always seemed so nice. He treated Maddie like a princess. How could he turn out like that?"

I tightened my grip on Kate's hand and guided her around a dead horseshoe crab that had washed onto the beach. "Pickron thinks Brett got greedy. Merritt said Brett was running the boat when they made the one-time haul of Panama Red. Brett stashed a couple of bales somewhere for safe keeping and tossed 'em overboard into the grass flats behind the Trade Winds. The next day when he went to retrieve the bales, he only found one. You know about the other bale that was found later, washed up on the island.

"And when the Panama Red started showing up around the area schools, it didn't take much figuring on Ben Merritt's part to realize why the inventory was a couple of bales short. Merritt delivered the organization's message of displeasure to Brett, and that's when he decided to skip town with Maddie and the money he'd made from the Panama Red. Problem was, Clayton Barfield wasn't the kingpin of the organization; somebody up north was. So, when Brett decided to heist a couple of bales for his own little operation, he was into the big boys for a bundle. There was no way he could come up with that kind of money."

Kate sighed. "So it wasn't just a romantic elopement they had planned, was it? Brett was running away from trouble and dragging Maddie into it."

"Yeah, but I believe he really did love Maddie, and because she was pregnant I think they planned on getting married soon. But before they could leave town, Brett and Maddie had their confrontation with Lamar, and that ended that." I wasn't convinced the marriage part was true, but for Kate's sake it seemed like the proper thing to say.

Kate stopped. She wedged a toe beneath a live starfish that had washed ashore and flipped it back into the surf. "That's why Lamar put Maddie's body behind the Trade Winds, isn't it? He wanted to throw suspicion off of him and make it look like her death was related to the drug smuggling. And that's why he sent you there to fish, hoping you'd find her body. And then he told you to try The Stumps and sent you that message about staying out of the water, didn't he? He wanted you to find Brett's boat. Dang it, Mac, he was trying to throw the blame off of him and onto you the whole time."

I pulled Kate close and gave her a big hug. "Come on," I said, taking her hand and leading her back up the beach toward the truck. "We've got a trip to plan."

ACKNOWLEDGMENTS

Many thanks to Karen, the best wife, friend, beta reader, critic, and editor a guy could be blessed with, for all the many hours invested and words of encouragement; to Fred Tribuzzo of the Rudy Agency, my friend and agent, who always goes above and beyond the call of duty; to Edward Stratemeyer, creator of *The Hardy Boys*, and Franklin W. Dixon, who in his many guises first piqued my interest in mysteries and provided untold hours of adventure and pleasure to a young dreamer.

ABOUT THE AUTHOR

A native of Georgia, E. Michael Helms grew up in Panama City, Florida, an area renowned for having the "world's most beautiful beaches." Helms turned down a chance to play college baseball and joined the Marine Corps after high school graduation. He served as a rifleman with the Second Battalion, Fourth Marine Regiment during some of the fiercest fighting of the Vietnam War, and was awarded the Purple Heart medal for wounds received in action. Helms's memoir of Vietnam, *The Proud Bastards*, has been called "as powerful and compelling a battlefield memoir as any ever written . . ." and has been in print for over twenty years. Helms is also the author of the two-part Civil War saga *Of Blood and Brothers*, and he is working on future volumes of the Mac McClellan Mystery series. He is the father of two daughters, and "Granddaddy Mike" to grandsons Liam and Levi. He and his wife live in the foothills of the Blue Ridge Mountains in the Upstate of South Carolina. For more information, visit him online at www.emichaelhelms.com and at www.facebook.com/EMichaelHelms.